THE KARMA CLEANER

D1739096

JOE GORMAN

ISBN: 1544075138
ISBN 13: 9781544075136
Library of Congress Control Number: 2017903568
CreateSpace Independent Publishing Platform
North Charleston, South Carolina

This is a work of fiction. Any resemblance to actual persons, living or dead, is purely coincidental. However, the town of Gloucester City, with its rich history, is fertile ground for stories and legends, some of which are true.

*Dedicated to my beautiful sweet angel, Joanne Convery Gorman.
I love you always and forever*

Visit Joe Gorman at his website josephpatrickgorman.com
Visit his Author Page, Joe Gorman, on Facebook
Please add him on Twitter @Joejoegorman
Add him on Instagram at josephpatrickgorman

John Oxley played alto sax in the Gloucester High concert band. He didn't play in the marching band because he was the third string halfback for the varsity football team, having carried the ball a whopping seven times in varsity competition by the end of his junior year. His carries were in games that were so lopsided that the outcome had long since been determined. But his presence on the football team gave him unmatched street cred in the band room. No one could remember another band member at Gloucester High who had played football.

He was a gifted musician, not only talented but someone who practiced enthusiastically 365 days a year. He was also an excellent student. Oxley was completely at home in the family-like atmosphere of the band room. He was built more like a yoga devotee than a running back. Despite his apparent lack of athleticism, he was admired and welcomed by the football coaching staff because he was enthusiastic and disciplined, and he worked hard every day. He tutored teammates who were marginal students. The coaches respected Oxley's work ethic and respect for the game.

Privately, he nurtured secret fantasies of athletic conquests. His daydreams often involved long runs from scrimmage and improbable one-handed catches in the end zone (despite not having caught a single pass in three seasons on the junior varsity squad). Would he trade his musical and academic gifts for the glory of athletic stardom? Sometimes he wondered.

Oxley was the concert band's first chair sax player. The band director said that he was the finest horn player the school had produced during his forty-year tenure. His only true peer in the band was a pianist, his classmate Barb Gambardello. The concert band was the pride of the school's music program. Barb was in the same AP classes as Oxley and ate lunch with him every day.

Barb changed her hair color with each new moon. She had King Crimson and Tool tattoos on her arms although she no longer listened to either band. Her bedroom floor was littered with Robert Crumb comic books, excerpts from Anaïs Nin's diaries, and photographs of Corgis she found online. Her skin was a whiter shade of pale and she was fascinated by Black literature, having read the Chester Himes and Ishmael Reed catalogs several times. Barb was a brilliant writer in the short forms popularized by social media, writing nothing longer each day than a paragraph commenting on an Instagram photo. Her social media feeds drew hundreds of Likes each day, and she was more popular on social media than at the high school.

Oxley and Barb planned to attend college together and major in music. During the summer before senior year, they practiced every morning in the school's concert band room to prepare to audition. They hoped to attend Rutgers because Barb's favorite pianist, Kenny Barron, was on the faculty. They met midway between their houses at 9 every morning and walked the remaining half mile to the high school together. They rehearsed two songs by alto sax legend Jackie McLean that they would use to audition. Barb was mystified that Oxley wanted to continue playing football for the high school despite his ambitious music plans.

"Why don't you just drop the whole football fantasy?" she asked. "Can you imagine how awesome you'd be if you concentrated on nothing but music? You'd be an unstoppable force, dude."

"You just hate jocks."

"I don't hate jocks. I hate 'games' that are violent and pointless."

"They're not pointless. Sports draws something out of me that I can't access in any other way."

"Like what? A head injury?"

"It makes you find out what's really inside you—what's real and what's fantasy. If you fail at grabbing it one day, you get more determined to bring it to the surface the next."

"Oxley, you're an amazing musician, but people say you're not particularly good at football."

"That's besides the point. Or maybe it *is* my point; that I access inner qualities that don't come up in the classroom— courage, stamina, resilience, the willingness to withstand discomfort to achieve a goal. They make me more expansive. Playing the sax and playing football both make me use my body for something other than supporting my head. I lose myself for a while. My thoughts shut off."

"Whatever you say, Oxley."

They were rehearsing a song called "I'll Keep Loving You," a lovely melody written by Bud Powell and energized by some provocative upper register alto sax in McLean's arrangement. The horn solos made Powell's languorous melody sound innovative and bold. Barb and Oxley were patient with each other's missteps and had good synergy. Their auditions were on October 16 at the Mason Gross School of Performing Arts in New Brunswick, but they could practice together only until football practice began in mid-August. Oxley and Barb treated the morning practices as essential, serious obligations and walked home together afterwards.

"Oxley, what's your projected career trajectory this morning?"

"Let me see. I'll start playing small clubs around New York City right after graduating from Rutgers. I want to be part of the second great Bebop revival. I'll get spotted by Questlove and get invited to the next D'Angelo recording session at the new Electric Ladyland studio. I become the go-to alto sax guy on either coast and record with Erykah Badu, Solange, and Childish Gambino. Finally, I play on the final Sly Stone masterpiece. What do you think?"

"I'll lay a thousand to one odds against."

"What's your projected career trajectory this week?"

"Think I might begin by recording the Eliane Elias songbook."

"So you'll get played on NPR radio twice a week and earn eight grand a year," Oxley laughed.

"Or I might just take voice lessons and go the Regina Spektor route."

"I vote for that."

They made plans to meet at 7 that evening at Barb's. They walked down Johnson Boulevard until Oxley turned left on Hudson Street and Barb continued walking past the Little League fields and the municipal basketball courts, across a small concrete hump bridge over a fetid swamp, and down Nicholson Road to her house. Barb lived in the Gloucester Heights section of the city. Most of the streets in the Heights were named after prominent universities: Oxford, Harvard, Yale, Dartmouth, Cornell—ironic, given the town's blue-collar roots. Barb's dad was a long-haul truck driver who apparently had peddled amphetamines to other truckers as a side gig. Her father purchased a large quantity of the pills from a man who was cooperating with the police to alleviate his own legal difficulties and was busted moments after pulling out of a motel parking lot. The motel was in Delaware, so her father was sentenced to three to five years in the James T. Vaughn Correctional Center in Smyrna. He was ashamed to let his daughter visit him in prison, so Barb had not seen him in three years. She wrote to him every month and he occasionally wrote back.

Barb created art in a multitude of forms. She collaged photos from magazines, superimposing '60s rock lyrics over kaleidoscopes of photos of Corgis, horses, clouds, and canyons. She painted and worked for months recreating Jim Marshall photographs of Janis Joplin on canvas. She couldn't work on ceramics at home, but pieces she made at school often filled the display cases lining the high school foyer. Barb's Design and Illustration teacher urged her to consider a career as a graphic artist, and Barb was invariably the high school "Artist of the Month" each September. If Barb wasn't so committed to creating music, she could have competed for scholarships to art school; she was *that* talented.

Oxley ran sprints and lifted weights every day in preparation for football season. Preseason practices began in two weeks. Oxley put his sax in his bedroom closet, grabbed a bottle of water and his spikes, and headed down Gaunt Street to the town's youth football fields. The football fields were behind the youth baseball fields, a sports complex that served kids ages five to ten. By the time he arrived at the football fields, he was a hundred yards away from the street, affording him the privacy mediocre athletes need to work out in earnest. Oxley ran sprints and used the youth teams' ladders to do some agility drills. The August heat was oppressive. Barb went to the fields with him a week earlier to time him in the 40-yard dash with her cell phone. The best time he ran was a 5.1. He trained hard to become as fast as his slow-twitch muscle fibers would allow.

After thirty minutes of sprints and agilities, Oxley walked five blocks to the city's Police Athletic League building to lift weights. The local police had converted a disused brick grammar school into an adequate fitness facility. They offered weight lifting, martial arts classes, and yoga classes taught in the evening by two of the cops' wives. A blacktop basketball court stood behind the building. Oxley preferred lifting at the PAL to lifting at the high school weight room. The football team lifted in the mornings which conflicted with his audition practices. He was grateful that he had an alternative place to lift each day. The PAL Club weight room was better equipped than the high school's. It was used by the local police officers, their friends, and people who were too old or too young to use the high school facility. The atmosphere was supportive and friendly, and the cops were glad to spot for the young lifters. They didn't hesitate to provide advice. They encouraged Oxley, asked questions about his music, and served as father figures to him and many others. Many of the cops were dedicated lifters. Oxley had followed a program devised by the football coaches and was finally bench pressing his own body weight.

Gloucester High had a long, proud tradition of fielding state powerhouses in football, basketball, softball, cross country, and field hockey. No team evoked more passion than the football team. Gloucester had frequently beaten bigger schools with better athletes through hard-nosed toughness and tenacity. The team won dozens of Tri-County Conference football titles from the mid-1960s through the early 2000s with teams that were well coached and disciplined. They developed an early devotion to weight training and were held together by the small town cohesiveness of kids who have played together shoulder-to-shoulder since kindergarten.

But lately the unthinkable had happened. The football fortunes of the mighty Gloucester Lions had slipped, slid, and then slid further. The spread offenses popular in the twenty-first century emphasized speed and athleticism and negated the grit and toughness of the Gloucester kids. It didn't matter how tough they were; they couldn't guard receivers in the open field or contain superior athletes playing quarterback and operating from the shotgun. No amount of grit could make up for their lack of foot speed and agility. The coaches, players, and fans were frustrated. The kids redoubled their efforts in the weight room, committed to summer workouts like never before, and went to overnight football camps, all to no avail. During the past ten years, if the Gloucester team finished the season above .500, it was considered a success. The bitterest pill to swallow, the true and real calamity of the past ten years occurred each Thanksgiving Day, the day of the traditional City Series game against crosstown rival Gloucester Catholic. The more reasonable Lions fans had come to accept that modern offenses favored the athletes from Salem, Glassboro, Clayton, and Penns Grove. Even casual fans could see how much quicker and fleeter those opponents were. What really brought pain and ignominy to the Gloucester teams was losing ten years in a row to the hated Rams. The Catholic kids didn't appear to be any different than the Gloucester kids—not quicker, not faster, not superior in any way that could be measured with a stop watch or on the weight bench. There was simply no logical explanation for it, and it ate at the pride of the townspeople.

The rival high schools had played the Thanksgiving game for the past eighty-seven years. Thousands of fans filled

John A. Lynch stadium every year for the 10:30 kickoff. And every year for the past decade, the Lions fans walked out with their heads down, sometimes by the end of the third quarter. The game cast a pall on many families' Thanksgiving dinners. A number of families had one parent who had attended Gloucester Catholic and another who had attended Gloucester High. The contests were observed with lighthearted spirits when the game was a toss-up every year. Gloucester had held a 43-34 winning edge at one point in the rivalry, but the Rams had now gained a 44-43 advantage.

The Gloucester High–Gloucester Catholic game would have even more significance this year for both squads because an administrative law judge had suspended post-season play-offs until the state athletic association implemented a system to regulate student transfers. Regular-season games would be the sole determinant of football superiority.

The head coach, Lee Claiborn, was a legendary Lions quarterback who led Gloucester to three consecutive undefeated seasons and then played in four major postseason bowl games in college. He had the same positive impact on the program as a coach. He was the winningest football coach in Gloucester history, but his stock had slipped in some corners because of the recent slide. Coach Claiborn and his staff worked harder than ever. The players worked harder than ever. But the losses on Thanksgiving continued. Any time a Gloucester football player ran into Lions alumni at Wawa, at one of the fishing piers, or a barbecue, the question was always asked: "Think we can beat the Rams this year?"

JOE GORMAN

After working out, Oxley showered, read a couple of chapters of Ken Kesey's *Sometimes a Great Notion*, and practiced the sax for an hour. He walked to Joe's Pizzeria at Broadway and Mercer Street, sat at the counter, and ordered a pizza steak for dinner. Oxley's mom was a Food Safety/Preventive Control supervisor at Holt Logistics and worked the 3 to 9 shift, six nights a week. As a consequence, Oxley ate dinner at Joe's two hundred evenings a year. Joe's was now owned by Joe's son, Nick. If Nick liked you, he added the suffix "boy" or "girl" to the end of your name. If Nick didn't like you, he didn't talk to you. Nick's close friends called him "Nicky-boy." Nick called Oxley "Oxley-boy." Your name was often the end of the conversation with the taciturn owner, so the greeting was treasured.

Nick was a man of few words and even less patience. His pizza was the best in South Jersey, made Sicilian-style but with the cheese on the bottom and the gravy on top. Nick had a world-weary, gruff manner and a kind heart. He never turned anyone away who came in and asked for a handout, but if a paying customer cleared his throat once with impatience when Nick was making a sandwich, Nick would turn his head slowly and give him such an evil eye that he never tried to rush Nick again. He asked for no quarter and gave none.

A group of old-time Gloucester guys had breakfast there every morning: Pop Sullivan, Ott Romeo, Nick Brown, Bob Cooney, Bud Lindsay, and Bill and Jim Yula. The regulars got up early every morning more for the opportunity to break each other's stones than for the cold cereal, oatmeal, bacon, and

10

eggs. Nick began making dough at 7 each morning. He had a Hobart L800 pizza dough mixer with a sixty-quart bowl in which he mixed flour, yeast, olive oil, salt, and sugar for hours to prepare enough dough to get through the day. Nick also diced onions, cut tomatoes, and shredded lettuce for the day's sandwiches. He arranged long hot peppers on baking sheet, drizzled olive oil over them, and seasoned them with salt, pepper, and garlic. He made a fresh tuna salad every morning and disposed of any leftover tuna salad from the day before. He cut provolone cheese and American cheese. He sliced very rare, wafer-thin ribeye for a day's supply of steak sandwiches. He mixed ground beef, eggs, bread crumbs, cayenne pepper, garlic, and Worcestershire sauce in large bowls to make hamburger patties. He accepted delivery of fresh baked rolls from Aversa's Bakery. He sliced lunch meat for hoagies. Nick was there every morning for four hours before the place opened for lunch at 11.

One day, someone noticed the light on and went in to keep him company. A few weeks later, somebody joined the first guy, then somebody else, then somebody else, and the next thing Nick knew, he was serving breakfast. Nick wouldn't serve anyone else breakfast but his friends. If someone walked in off the street and sat at the counter, Nick would say, "We're not open for breakfast," despite the presence of six to ten Gloucester guys sitting in the booths eating breakfast.

Joe's had a jukebox from the 1960s that gave you six plays for a quarter; the records had not been changed in nearly fifty years. A vending company that owned the jukebox went out of business and never returned to remove it from the pizzeria. Oxley played "Hush" by Deep Purple, "A Double Shot of My Baby's Love" by the Swinging Medallions, "I Wish It Would Rain" by the Temptations, "Nobody But Me" by the Human Beinz, "Forever" by the Marvelettes, and "Sally Sayin' Something" by Billy Harner. Fifteen minutes of analog bliss, a cheese steak smothered in pizza gravy, and everyone left you alone—Joe's was Oxley's favorite spot in the universe. Oxley fed the jukebox another nickel, listened to James Brown's "There Was a Time," and then headed to Barb's.

Barb was on her computer looking for inspiration for her next tattoo. Her mom was rarely home in the evenings because she worked as ER nurse from at Our Lady of Lourdes Hospital in Camden, dealing with gunshot wounds, drug overdoses, the chronically mentally ill, and pregnant, frightened fourteen-year-olds. Her mom worked the second shift, Monday through Friday. Barb claimed that her mom was "traumatized by the trauma she sees every night." Barb had told Oxley that her mom and her "used to be close." Oxley asked her when, and Barb said, "when I was breastfeeding."

Barb and Oxley planned to work on a project for AP Anatomy, a course they would be taking for senior science. All AP courses involved workshops, independent reading, group projects, and work packets. They spent four afternoons during July in the science lab reviewing the project guidelines with their teacher. Barb and Oxley chose "An Interactive Display Introducing Histology" as their summer project. The teacher helped them with the project design. They accessed the necessary lab tools and instrumentation, took copious notes, asked questions, and gained project approval. They were required to summarize their lab findings and construct an interactive display that illustrated the microscopic structure of organic tissue. They grew interested in the project and worked on it with some enthusiasm. After two hours working at Barb's kitchen table on "The Minute Structure, Composition, and Function of African Violet Tissues," they headed to her bedroom to listen to record albums.

They were analog snobs and listened only to vinyl records. They hated compressed musical files and swore that music recorded straight to digital lacked the warmth of analog recordings. But they remained in willful denial for the sake of Sufjan Stevens. They loved his music and had watched the YouTube performance of "The Owl and the Tanager" so many times that Barb once calculated that they had spent an entire day of their lives watching it. They boasted so much about listening only to analog music that they were forced to listen to Sufjan surreptitiously. Barb owned the entire Sufjan Stevens catalog on vinyl and put *Carrie & Lowell* on the turntable. They always sat shoulder to shoulder with their backs against the side of her bed. Barb had a Pioneer PL-12D II turntable, a Sansui 771 receiver, and a pair of small Advent speakers sitting on a dresser facing the side of her bed. The music was restorative, healing. Barb got up to switch the record to the B side and when she sat back down, Oxley kissed her on the forehead.

"Hold on a minute—Am I dreaming, or did you just kiss me tenderly on the forehead?"

"I might have."

"Was it meant to be romantic, or something a boy would do to his little sister if she skinned her knee?"

"It felt romantic."

"Annnnnnddddddd??????????"

"It felt appropriate and romantic. But I don't want to mess up our friendship because it's the best thing, by far, I've got going in my life."

He started rubbing his index finger in gentle patterns on her forehead.

"Do you have a forehead fetish or is there a chance you might kiss me in other places some day?"

Oxley kissed her gently on the lips.

"Dude, you're blowing my mind. And making me happy. Do you know how many times I wished for this moment to happen? It feels like a dream. And my dreams don't usually come true."

"Let's not let this be one more thing we just talk about until we've analyzed the life out of it," Oxley said. "Why can't we ever just stay in the flow, stay in our bodies? We always immediately redirect everything to our head for analysis. Let's just not let it mess anything up…."

Barb tossed her eyeglasses on the bed and began to kiss him. Both of their faces were red from the sudden excitement. It didn't go farther than kissing that night, but they spent the next fifteen minutes with Barb draped across Oxley's body, her arms around his neck. They heard Barb's mom unlocking the front door and quickly gathered themselves. Barb put her glasses back on and smoothed her hair, miming, "Do I look all right?" before her mom stuck her head in and asked how they were doing.

"Why aren't you changing the record?" she asked. "It's stuck in the run-out groove."

Barb got up and flipped it back to the A side.

"If either of you guys is hungry, I've got some leftover salmon from dinner," she said and headed into the kitchen.

"I better get going," Oxley whispered.

"Why are you whispering?" she laughed.

"Still a little stunned," he said.

"Remember, we're not going to let this mess anything up."

She walked him to the door and he started heading down Nicholson Road toward Brown Street. Oxley felt like a gyroscope was spinning wildly in his head, that he had to wait for it to slow and regain his balance. When he entered his house, he looked and saw that he had received a text from Barb.

"And what love can do, that dares love attempt."

"Can't wait to see you tomorrow," he replied.

The following morning they walked to the high school to rehearse. They handled the situation exactly as you might expect. They didn't hold hands. They didn't give each other a quick peck on the lips. They didn't discuss what had transpired. They ignored it and proceeded as if nothing had happened. They had so many secrets from the rest of the world, they felt like they were enclosed in a bubble anyway. Both were grateful it hadn't changed their dynamic. Barb put her sheet music on the piano, and Oxley adjusted the reed on his sax.

"Are you sure you want to do that 'Melonae' number for Rutgers? All that screeching might be risky. That's Jackie McLean exposing his soul. He'd been through a whole lot more than you. They might not feel it's authentic coming from you," Barb said.

"Why do you always come up with these things?"

"Because I'm not on a Jackie McLean trip like you. I know you love the guy, but that song seems too personal. I'm not sure how they'll take it."

"I'll think about it. Let's just practice the other one today."

"Don't be sore. I'm telling you the truth. You're getting one shot at impressing Rutgers. Maybe you should show them how great you paint inside the lines before you show them the stuff you can do outside the lines."

"I wish there was a way I could show them that I can play in and out. That I will be fine in an ensemble but capable of really blowing, of being a leader."

"Well, 'I'll Keep Loving You' is a masterpiece. You do it so well. We're going to slay it. We're halfway there and we still have a few months to practice."

They practiced for ninety minutes before Barb had to leave to audition for the high school drama production of *Noises Off.*

Oxley walked home alone. As he rounded the edge of the high school driveway to cross Market Street, a short, stocky, reddish faced man who appeared to be in his fifties approached from a grove of fir trees that served as a buffer between the high school and the steady automobile traffic along Market Street. The man wore an Alabama Crimson Tide t-shirt and tan khakis. He had the mischievous energy of an adolescent, a taut face, and the swagger of a high school gym teacher who flattered himself by thinking he could still kick anyone's ass in the building. He wore a baseball cap that read "Loose lips sink ships," and when he removed it momentarily to rub his scalp, the man's hair was so fine it looked like it would blow off his head in a stiff breeze. His teeth were yellowing and a bit crooked in spots, the neglect of an alpha male who planned to win the day with his backslapping, rough-housing energy rather than his looks. He looked like he hadn't ever reflected on whether or not he was handsome; being tough enough to run the show in the locker room was enough. Oxley crossed

Market Street, and the man quickened his pace to walk alongside him down Greenwood Avenue.

"The chick with the crazy hair is right. That one Jackie McLean number is out of your league, junior. Try a Jazz Messengers piece or something for the second number. They're going to think all that wailing is either too precious or too crazy. You're biting off more than you can chew. You're no Jackie McLean."

"Excuse me, do I even know you? What were you doing snooping around outside the music room? Kinda creepy, dude."

"Nah, music's not really my thing. You can play 'Lollipop' by Lil Wayne for all I care. I'm a sports guy. A trainer. I'm the guy who just might save you from being a four-year JV guy. I can adjust your football potential like no one else on the planet. No spotlight is brighter than the sports spotlight, my brother. Believe me, I know."

Oxley stopped as they approached Martin's Lake.

"Who the heck are you? How do you even know about me?"

"Research, my man. I've been in R&D since before most people even realized it existed."

"Dude, I get little enough respect around here without people seeing me hanging out with a middle-aged guy in a Crimson Tide t-shirt. No offense, but why don't you go see if any of the kids fishing at the lake need a trainer?"

"All right, Jackie McLean. See you around. Don't forget what I said about how I can help you realize your football potential. In just a few lessons, you'll realize potential you don't even realize you have. I guess that's what they say about all great teachers and coaches, right? I see potential in you that other people haven't yet. Give me a chance to optimize your abilities."

Oxley was bemused. He had a difficult time believing he had any latent athletic ability that hadn't already been realized. He put his sax away, grabbed a bottle of water, and headed right to the fields on Johnson Boulevard. He walked down Mercer Street, crossed Johnson, skipped over the railroad tracks, walked past the tee ball fields, and hopped the fence to the football field. He walked over to lay his water bottle on the aluminum bleachers and noticed the guy in the Crimson Tide shirt sitting five rows up.

"Awww, c'mon, man! You're not going to tell me you're my long lost deadbeat dad or something, are you? What can you possibly want from me?"

Oxley grabbed his water bottle and headed to the PAL Club to lift. He'd come back later and run. He'd ask the cops if they knew anything about the guy in the Alabama shirt. The guy started walking beside him.

"Just give me ten minutes, junior. I'll stay on one side of the fence and you stay on the other. You might be slow but if you can't outrun me you'd be pathetic. I can almost guarantee you'll see improvements you never dared to dream. It'll take five minutes. If you still are unsettled, I will disappear and you'll never see me again."

Oxley put his water bottle back on the bleachers.

"There's no physical contact involved. I'll watch you run and then give you some pointers. You just might be the guy to lead the Lions back to their glory days. Probably something you're already hoping for."

"My dreams are all about becoming a musician."

"Do you even believe that stuff? That's the dream you settled for because better dreams seemed out of reach. But I'm going to put them within your reach."

"But my dreams really *are* about music."

"Junior, if that was really the case, you wouldn't be out here in the August sun trying to prove something to somebody. You'd be home working on your embouchure or something. The music career sounds like some hazy idea your mom planted in your head because your grandpop's band opened up for Hall and Oates once in the '60s. Seemed like a safe enough dream. Or maybe you got sucked into your friend Lady Gaga's dream. So you've become a supporting actor in her dream because your own real dreams seem so far away. There's probably not a lot of demand in the business world for chicks who change their hair color every three days, so what other option does she have except music? But I'm going to give you other options. Time to stop wandering around in other people's dreams and ignite one of your own."

"What can I possibly do two weeks before practice starts that will make any significant difference in my performance? I'm pretty sure I've already maximized whatever slender athletic benefits my genes gave me. Even my Anatomy textbook rubs the truth in my face: 'slow-twitch muscle fibers contract slowly, are relatively better at resisting fatigue, and provide endurance rather than strength.'"

"Slow-twitch, fast-twitch, it's all the same to me, junior. I'm operating at a different level. I will turbo boost those muscle fibers of yours and twitch them toward Jim Brown territory. You know who Jim Brown is?"

"No."

"Great, you've got some homework to do. Want me to assign a paper on him so you'll have something to do tonight besides hanging out at Gaga's?"

"What's the regimen involve? I don't want to be taking human growth hormone or anything. Not even steroids. I'm not desperate."

"Actually we're all pretty desperate, junior. You might be surprised. Do you know how desperate some of the people in this town are to beat Gloucester Catholic? In this town, every time you come back to visit your mom, people will want to talk about your high school football legacy—or lack of legacy in your case. And what's your legacy going to be? Remember that time you fell on the onside kick in the JV game against Wildwood? You might as well give up now if *that's* going to be the high-water mark. But I can change all that. Every time you come back to visit, you'll be hailed as the greatest, most improbable gridiron hero this sports-crazy town's ever seen. You'll never pay for a beer in this town if you live to be a hundred."

"Give me the specifics and I'll tell you if I'm interested."

"Well, let's start by timing you in the forty. I didn't bring a calendar with me, so there's no sense timing you in anything longer."

"Not funny, dude. What's your name, anyway? Old Scratch?"

"Ah, 'The Devil and Tom Walker.' Washington Irving. Still have to read that nineteenth-century crap in American Lit? I hated everything until we got to the Romantics. I'm in the redemption business. Redemption and reclamation. My name's McGrogan, Bill McGrogan."

"I already know my time in the forty. My friend timed me. It's a little over five seconds."

"Let's run one more time for all the old times, okay, junior? Just humor me. Then we'll make a few adjustments and see if you notice any difference."

McGrogan stood on the old aluminum bleachers with a handheld silver watch that a cross country coach in the 1950s may have used. Oxley knelt into a sprinter's stance at the 30-yard line, shook his shoulders a few times to release some tension, and burst into a full sprint until he reached the opposing 30-yard line. He trotted a few yards until he caught his breath and turned and walked back to the fence that separated the field from the bleachers.

"You ever think about converting to a lineman?" McGrogan asked.

"You're hilarious. How fast was I?"

"How slow were you? Too slow to be an effective high school running back without the Dallas Cowboys offensive line blocking for you."

Oxley walked in a tight circle and spit a few times.

"What can be done at this point?'

"There's a lot that can be done. All we have to do is overcome weak genetics, inefficient running form, and lack of proper training. That shouldn't be too hard."

"What can I do?"

"Come over to the fence. There's a region of your sternum that needs an adjustment. It's called the xiphoid process."

"Huh?"

"The human sternum is shaped like a necktie. There's a crucial part along the bottom called the xiphoid process. It can be adjusted to great advantage. Some truly wise people, yogis in ancient India, realized this a long time ago.

I have to touch you lightly on the chest and make a quick adjustment. It's quick, painless and noninvasive. Step over to the fence for a minute."

Oxley walked skeptically to the fence. McGrogan touched the middle of Oxley's sweaty t-shirt and pushed his thumb and three longest fingers into the lower sternum.

"All done."

"Dude, is this one of those prank shows? You've got to be kidding me."

"Go ahead. Get back out on the field and try running another 40. The first time you ran a 5.2. That's concert band speed. If you want to be a football guy, give me one chance. Go ahead. See if you notice any difference."

Oxley hesitated but went back and resumed a sprinter's stance at the 30. He blasted off the line and reached the other 30 in a flash. He finished before the usual waves of self-doubt appeared. He finished before he realized he was running. He jogged back to the fence.

"Dude, what just happened? I was running so fast I felt unconscious!"

"You were in the zone, brother. You went from a 5.2 to a 4.5 in one easy lesson. It helps that you're slender. Big muscular guys are hampered by wind resistance. Not many running backs are as thin as you, but you're going to be quick enough to avoid most hits at the high school level. Joe McKnight was a great running back at USC and he was slender. Imagine you getting compared to Joe McKnight!"

"What's the catch, dude? Why me, of all people?"

"Well, as they say, son, the devil's in the details. Let's meet for dinner at Joe's Pizzeria this evening at four thirty. You can buy me one of those pizza steaks. But I want you to think about this in the meantime. I can help you become not just the best running back in Gloucester; you can become the best running back in New Jersey. With you in the backfield, the Lions will be good enough to run the table like in the old days. You might go into the Gloucester Catholic game as a heavy favorite. When's the last time that happened? The year after Woodstock? That old Gloucester spirit would be rejuvenated. They might even erect a statue of you one day. Sounds like a lot more fun than playing the horn, doesn't it? Access your inner man. Take another path for a while. Maybe even settle a few scores."

"And the catch is? And the details are?"

"Let's go over that stuff at dinner. See you at four thirty. I heard they have a decent juke box. I'll bring a few nickels."

Oxley watched McGrogan walk away, gathered his towel and water bottle, and headed to the PAL Club. Walking along the railroad tracks toward Somerset Street felt surreal. Thoughts flooded his mind. Did he really want to be a football star? Is that why he stayed with it these past three years despite being discouraged by Barb, humbled at practice, and ignored at home? For the chance to stand out at something valued by the majority of students and towns people? Is he that insecure about who he is? Why does he want the respect people who don't really know him?

He told himself that it was an illusion that he was running fast. Maybe he just forgot about all of the crippling self-doubt that haunted him even on short runs so it felt like he finished faster. Maybe McGrogan was lying about the time. Of course! He blushed from the realization that he had gone along with this silly fantasy and walked through the gate of the PAL Club.

He walked up the steep steps of the former elementary school and pressed the doorbell. The door buzzed open and he walked down to the weight room on the basement level. Oxley was as impulsive as any other adolescent and started loading weight on the bar of the bench press. He normally put a thirty-five-pound weight and 2 ten-pound weights on each side and warmed up with two sets of ten lifts before taking the ten-pound weights away and pairing a twenty-five-pound weight with the thirty-five-pound weight on each side. He would do two sets of ten lifts with the additional weight. On days that he wanted to max out, he would add a small 2.5-pound weight on each side to bench his body weight, 170 pounds.

He was disoriented about his encounter with McGrogan at the youth football field and curious to see if the so-called adjustment McGrogan made had led to any increase in body strength. He would be able to empirically measure any gain in strength on the weight bench. So today he put 2 thirty-five-pound weights on the bar. He laid on the bench and a cop named Murphy walked over from the lat machine to spot him.

"You always lift this much weight, John?" he asked.

"To be honest, no. But I want to prove something to myself, so will you spot me for a minute? I'm probably not going to get it more than a few inches off the rack."

"Sure. Don't strain too much. I had a hernia operation two summers ago and I really think the cause of that problem was the result of my stupidity on the weight bench when I was younger. There's no need to impress anyone here. The surest way to prevent any injuries is to stick to the program. There's a science to it. I thought you appreciated that."

"I do. I'll give it one shot and if I start straining, will you just let it back down on the rack?'

"Give it one try."

Oxley laid on the bench and got his feet into optimal position to assist in the lift. He had a nervous habit of arching his back a few time before attempting any heavy lift. He breathed deeply and tried to keep his mind calm. He grunted and lifted the bar until his arms were fully extended. It was fifteen pounds heavier than he had ever lifted before. He let the weight bar slowly descend to his chest, pushed it up until his arms were extended, let it down, pushed it up; after ten reps, he stopped.

"Impressive, buddy. You've made some major improvements since I last spotted you," Murphy said.

"Can I try to add a five and a two-and-a-half to each side to see if I can get up two hundred?" he asked.

"I guess," Murphy said. "Just don't get carried away. Respect your limits and you'll stay healthy enough that you'll have new max lifts soon. Don't overdo it."

Oxley put the weights on and refastened the clamp at each end. He went through his routine of flattening his feet until he felt they were perfectly placed, arched his back, focused on his breathing, grunted, and then lifted the bar up and down three times in rapid succession.

"You taking steroids?" Murphy asked, grinning. "I thought you were the Honor Roll kid who was a musician. You really packed on the strength this summer. I didn't bench press two hundred pounds until college."

"I've been doing this program with some guy I met," Oxley said.

"Looks like it's working, buddy," Murphy said and walked back to the lat pulldown bench. Oxley grabbed his water bottle and sprinted up the stairs and out the door. He couldn't wait to see McGrogan later.

Oxley went home and showered. He practiced his sax for an hour but without his usual fervor, then walked to Joe's Pizzeria for dinner. Joe's had a long Formica counter on the left side of the restaurant and a row of wooden booths with that resembled shortened church pews on the right side, all vintage late '50s accoutrements. A grill and cash register were behind the counter. Nestled along the wall next to the grill were toasters, pale green milkshake mixers, cups, saucers, a cash register, a stainless steel sink, and wood framed photos of President Kennedy, Pope John XXIII, and Nick's parents. If you walked past the counter to the back of the restaurant, you passed the restroom and juke box before arriving at a taller counter that separated the pizza kitchen from the restaurant. It was ten degrees warmer at the pizza counter with no seating. Large silver pizza ovens and another cash register were behind the counter. Oxley heard the strains of Canned Heat's "On the Road Again" as soon as he opened the door. He scanned the counter and found no sign of McGrogan. He walked toward the grill counter and sat down on one of four stools with faded red sparkle Naugahyde seats that lined the counter. He sat and waited only a second before he heard McGrogan's voice behind him croaking the lyrics to the Canned Heat song.

Oxley spun on the stool and faced McGrogan.

"How was the rest of your afternoon, my brother?" McGrogan asked.

"Dude, what is going on?"

"I love Canned Heat. What a jukebox! I could spend my entire salary in this place. Sit back and enjoy the music, junior. I can see why you love this place."

"Get real for a minute, McGrogan. What the heck did you do to me? I went to the PAL Club and benched two hundred pounds without breaking a sweat. I was afraid to put any more weight on the bar because it would've freaked out the cop who was helping me. Was 4.5 really my time in that forty-yard sprint?"

"Relax, big daddy. It could still come down another tenth of a second, maybe two tenths, before your season's over."

"But how do you explain the changes? You touched the outside of my t-shirt for five seconds and I'm a superior athlete? Who are you?"

"I'm the seventh son of a seventh son, my brother. But let's order a couple of those pizza steaks everyone talks about before we get down to business. I'm starving."

Oxley spun back to the counter and asked Nick to make two pizza steaks.

"Drinking anything?" Nick asked, glancing backwards from the grill.

"I'll take a diet soda and…"

"You got cream soda?" McGrogan asked.

"Only in a bottle," Nick replied.

"Gimme a bottle of cream soda."

Oxley waited for Nick to finish grilling a burger, took the sodas from him, and sat back down in the booth, pushing the bottle toward McGrogan.

"Junior, do you know that the Gloucester High Lions were so fierce in the late '60s, early '70s that people started referring to them as the Huns, without even a trace of irony? They must have had some teams."

"I heard about them. People still talk about them."

"They went three seasons without a single loss, right? Well, let's bring that shit back again. I love this town, and I'm tired of losing to Catholic."

"Who are you? Where are you from? How did you even know about me or about Gloucester?"

"I'm in a line of work I don't think you've ever heard of. I'm a Karma Cleaner. I've got a football-playing client who is in a big jam out West. He's gone and got himself suspended, deservedly so, for a nasty incident involving his girlfriend. He's suspended for a year and won't be needing his football ability for a while. But he will be needing your nerdish good karma because he's so scorned right now that he's repulsing people. He's radioactive. He can't go out and behave in a way that accumulates good karma. There isn't a soup kitchen, homeless shelter, anti-graffiti force, or any other do-good organization that would risk sullying their name by working with him. People would see it as desperate and insincere on his part. He wants to show that he's genuinely changed, and one quick way of doing that is through a good karma cleanse. People will at least be able to detect that he's vibrating at a higher level. He'll become a cute little puppy like you, amigo. Sounds a little New-Agey but there's actually some truth to it. And with some serious anger management counseling, psychotherapy, and making a committed effort to remain sober, maybe he'll grow into someone trustworthy. He's a brilliant running back."

"Why me?"

"Can you imagine how hard it was to find someone who is so clean living and nerdish that he's alone in a bedroom a hundred nights a year with a girl he's secretly in love with, not a sober adult in sight, and it takes him a year to get up the impulse to kiss her on the forehead? And who also nurtures secret dreams of being a football star? The equation looked like this:

$$\text{great karma} + \text{weak athletic ability} + \text{high athletic}$$
$$\text{aspirations} = \text{John Oxley.}"$$

"I'm not secretly in love with her."

"Then you're not-so-secretly in love with her, right?"

"Wrong."

"Ok, then you don't yet realize you're in love with her."

"And you couldn't find anyone else for the karma switch?"

"There's a baton twirler in Poughkeepsie who was a pretty close fit, but he broke his thumb in a dustup at band camp so that led me to Gloucester City, New Jersey, and you."

"What's the terms of the deal?'

"You sign a contract for having one hundred days of phenomenal athletic ability, national class foot speed, power, strength and agility; the football psycho gets the benefits of your good karma. After one hundred days, if you choose, you sign a long-term contract for more mutually agreed upon benefits. The one hundred-day tryout contract goes into effect tomorrow morning at ten thirty. You have until then to back out of the whole damned affair."

"And what if I want out after the hundred days are up?"

"Well, you'd be just in time to regain your rightful place in the Gloucester High School Lonely Hearts Club Band. No hard feelings either way, I hope."

"Do I have some time to think it over?"

"Yeah, until we finish these sandwiches and our soda. That should give you more than enough time to realize you'd be out of your mind not to become the best high school running back in New Jersey in exchange for your seventeen years of nerd karma. You won't lose a thing. You'll still be a terrific sax player, still be a good student, still be paling around with the Courtney Love wannabe. Although I've gotta tell you, junior, by the second scrimmage you might start thinking about trading up to someone a little sportier, someone who shaves her armpits regularly. But it's up to you. I'm sure you've heard the recovery room cliché—when you change the way you look at things, the things you look at change. Being an alpha athlete may change the way you look at things, that's all I'm saying. You sign it after dinner and it goes into effect tomorrow morning at ten thirty."

"Let's eat."

"Any chance the final decades of the twentieth century will ever arrive in Gloucester? Anybody doing location scouting for a movie set in the late '60s should check this place out," McGrogan said, looking around admiringly. "They don't even have to change anything on the jukebox. And they can use you and your girlfriend for the 'Who Killed Jazz?' segment of the Birth of Garage Rock scene shot right here at Joe's Pizzeria. Is this whole town stuck in the '60s, or just you and your girlfriend?"

"So after one hundred days I can go back to my old life completely, no strings attached? I'll be exactly who I am now?"

"Only more so, amigo, because if you want to crawl back into this life after feeling the excitement you're about to feel, you're getting enshrined into the Geek Hall of Fame."

"Ok, I'll go for it."

"Smart move, my brother. Let me give you a few pointers right out of the gate. Football starts tomorrow, right? Go slow at first. Don't try to impress anybody until you get closer to the season. You might show the proverbial 'flashes of brilliance,' but don't start flooring it until you adjust to driving with a bigger engine. It's going to feel strange for a little while. Give yourself some time to adjust."

"Won't be a problem. The coaches will start me off on the third string when practices begin. How will I get in touch with you if I have a question about anything?"

"I'll give you my cell number. You can text me any time you need me. Much as I'd like to see your girlfriend's stunning performance in *Noises Off,* I've got battles to fight and work to do. Been good knowing you, junior. Hope this is the start of a long and mutually profitable arrangement."

"For a hundred days, anyway."

"Completely up to you."

McGrogan went to the counter, paid for the sandwiches, and disappeared into the sultry August evening.

Oxley walked to Barb's. She was in the kitchen cleaning a record purchased at a yard sale. No music was too obscure for Barb; in fact, the less chance anyone else had ever heard of it increased the chance that Barb would like it. Hip kids at Gloucester High were into hip hop artists like Dillon Cooper, The Left, Felly, and Ant Beale. A few kids were '90s grunge freaks. There were plenty of metalheads wearing Slayer, Iron Maiden, and Anthrax t-shirts. The Beatles, Stones, and Kinks had plenty of followers. Dozens swore allegiance to Biggie and Tupac. All were too mainstream for Barb's taste. Anyone who has been played on commercial radio during the past twenty-five years was "the kind of artist they play on commercial radio." Barb didn't like people very much, and she didn't like artists whom other people liked. She was wiping a record by free jazz sax player Archie Shepp with great relish.

"Look what I found at some old guy's yard sale!" she said, waving a gatefold album cover entitled *Attica Blues* that featured a photo of Shepp sitting at a piano, cigarette dangling from his mouth, his sax laid across the piano, and his face completely absorbed in composing.

"It's on the Impulse label," further cementing the bonds of the secret society to which only she and Oxley belonged.

"Let's listen to it," Oxley said, "but first let me tell you about some guy I met today down the youth league fields who worked some kind of juju on me to make me a better football player."

"What??"

"I met some guy walking home after we rehearsed today and he knows some ancient practice where he can mystically reformulate someone's athletic potentialities…"

"Dude," Barb interrupted, "I hope you're messing with me, because you're really tripping if you're not. You didn't pay him any money, did you? Isn't athletic potential innate and limited?"

"He claims otherwise and sort of demonstrated to me that it's more malleable than people think."

"Oxley, I feel sorry for you. It'd be like me sitting here telling you I'm entering the Miss America Pageant because I met someone that transformed me into Beyoncé. Why don't you just face the reality that you're a super talented musician, smart as anybody, handsome, kind, independent, peaceful, and altogether lovely? Why isn't that enough? Why do you keep wanting the one thing you can't have? For who? For what?"

"It's how people get noticed. It's how boys get noticed, anyway. Do you really think anyone around here besides you appreciates my musical abilities? It's not like I'm a rapper or indie band singer. I play the saxophone."

"You're thinking like a boy. Who gives a hoot who notices you? It's people who have no idea who they are trying to tell you who you are."

"Anyway, it's too late now. I signed a deal with that guy. I've got some new abilities."

"Did you swallow some 'shrooms? You have some 'new abilities?' That's something one of the gamers at school says about fantasy video games. Like they've got a speed and stamina boost so now they'll survive the hail storm. You are really tripping."

"I know it sounds weird, but I lifted way more than normal at the PAL Club this afternoon. And remember when you timed me down the youth league fields? I cut about a second off my 40 time just like that."

"You're making my head spin, dude. Can we listen to a record?"

"Yes."

'Do you want me to put the record on the turntable like normal, or are you going to play it by telekinesis with your new powers?"

"Don't break my stones. I haven't even had time to absorb any of this. It all happened since our rehearsal this morning."

"Dude, you're giving me a headache."

Football practice began on August 16, with physicals and equipment distribution in the morning and practice from 3:00 until 6:00. Until concussion protocols were instituted, it was routine for high schools in New Jersey to have double sessions of practice the first two weeks of the new scholastic season.

Double sessions were banned in 2015 due to safety concerns. The concussion protocols are this specific: for the first two days of football practice, players can wear no equipment except helmets; for the next three days, shoulder pads are added; on the sixth day, teams can practice in full gear. Gloucester High provides free physicals to all fall athletes in the nurse's office for two days each summer. The boys and girls cross country teams, the boys and girls soccer teams, the field hockey team, and the football team are assigned time slots, and with the school nurse and athletic trainer assisting a local doctor, the physicals proceed smoothly and efficiently. Oxley was anxious about how the apparent changes in his genetic makeup might affect his blood pressure and resting pulse rate, but the doctor and nurse were blasé about the results. The equipment distribution went smoothly and included good-natured ribbing from the coaching staff about how there were bigger expectations on him this year. Oxley never had much to say, and he shrugged self-consciously. Oxley put his equipment in his football locker and walked to Wawa to grab something to eat before practice. He ran into Mr. and Mrs. Hodson, two of the most loyal Lions fans in the city.

"Playing football again this year, John?" Mrs. Hodson asked.

"Yeah, gonna give it one more shot."

"Hey, a lot of guys have really come into their own in their senior year, guys people hadn't really noticed too much when they were younger. Sometimes having older guys around is a bit intimidating to the quieter kids. This might be your breakout year, buddy. We'll be rooting for you."

"Thanks a lot. I appreciate it."

"Beat the Rams."

"We're gonna try."

Oxley crossed Market Street and walked along the school driveway back to the locker room. Gloucester High was a place that taught students to respect each other's differences, but there are always guys who are late getting the message. As soon as Oxley entered the locker room, a loud-mouthed senior named Ron Thones said, "Oxley. Can't believe your skinny ass is still on the team. Where you been all summer, marching band camp?"

Oxley ignored him but Thones continued.

"Why do you even bother coming out? Gonna be a bunch of sophomores getting more playing time than you. Give up and just be a manager. Go get me a bottle of water."

Thones embarrassed himself every time he opened his mouth. His teammates ignored him. He was big and powerfully built but never delivered results on the playing field that you might expect from a player of his size and strength. He had overpromised and underdelivered for three seasons, and there was no reason to expect that this year will be any different; that didn't stop him from bullying the underclassman, the scout teams, or anybody else he thought he could get away with intimidating any time the coaches were out of earshot. He was an unstable, volatile blowhard. Gloucester High had a two-suspension, no further extracurricular activities rule: if a student was given an out-of-school suspension twice during the same school year for discipline infractions, he was no longer eligible to participate in sports, attend dances, or be on school grounds for any reason after the school day. Consequently, Thones hadn't lasted past October during the past three seasons and was likely to be placed in the district Alternative School Program if he got into any trouble this year.

The rest of the team causally greeted each other and quietly dressed. It was time to get down to business after a summer of lifting, running sprints, and listening to the unreasonable expectations from family, friends. and neighbors. The coaches met in a room adjacent to the locker room. Coach Claiborn had quarterbacked the Lions during the most successful era in the program's history. They went 25-0-2 from 1969-1971. He was named the South Jersey Player of the Year in the *Philadelphia Inquirer.* He was smart, tough, and self-directed. He had track record as both a player and a coach that should have left him well above reproach. It didn't. He was arguably the greatest athlete in Gloucester City history. He was arguably the greatest coach in Gloucester history. That wasn't enough for the Lions fans. As unthinkable as it may have seemed ten years ago, Coach Claiborn was feeling the pressure. There were whispers that a younger coach may have a more organic understanding of the new spread offenses that proved so perplexing to Gloucester. Claiborn had played in the days of the Delaware wing T and split T. Some people whispered that the spread offenses popular in 2016 were not decipherable to an old-timer.

After dressing in their practice gear, the boys walked out past their fenced-in, well-manicured game day field to the crabgrass-strewn practice field behind it. The patch of crab-grass and dirt where the Lions practiced every day suited the character of their coach and the underdog aura that surrounded the Gloucester football program. A few players grabbed water bottles from a portable cart along the fence and the players knelt on one knee and Coach Claiborn addressed the team:

"It's great to see you guys. I'm proud of the commitment you made to training all summer, working around your summer jobs to get to the weight room, showing up for running sessions, and your commitment to turning this program back in the right direction, the winning direction. I know it's hot but it's hot for every team in South Jersey right now. It's mid-August. No one is practicing indoors. We're all working and sweating in this heat. There's plenty of water over there. Get a drink any time you need one. You guys know you don't have to ask. Know that it's your responsibility to stay hydrated. Drink plenty of water during the breaks. Our first character test of the season is dealing with the heat and not letting the heat defeat us. Starting tomorrow we'll practice in the mornings when it's cooler. We have to accept the fact that this town always has big expectations for us. We also have to accept the fact that we haven't met their expectations for some time now. We all have to accept the responsibility to turn this thing around. The coaches have never worked harder. We will work even harder during the season. I ask the same of you. Stay focused on what we have to do to become a better team and what you have to do to become a better player."

The players split up into offense, defense, and special teams. Kids were off to the side punting and place kicking. There was a line coach who worked with both the offensive and defensive linemen, an offensive coordinator who worked with the receivers at practice every day, a defensive coordinator who worked with the defensive backs and safeties, a special teams coach, and a coach who worked with the running backs. Coach Claiborn worked with the quarterbacks each day. The heat was sweltering but there was plenty of enthusiasm and energy. Every high school team was optimistic in August. Character tests were administered in October once teams sustained a few losses. In August, every team was undefeated and hoping to stay that way. Oxley worked with the running backs. There was no differentiation of ability levels during drills. Once intrasquad scrimmaging began, players would be placed on a depth chart which determined how many reps they'd get at practice. Oxley heeded McGrogan's advice and did nothing flashy or out of the ordinary. The coaches were happy to have him around but had no expectations other than the hope that his work habits might rub off on others. There was even some talk in the coaches room of naming Oxley one of the captains of this year's team.

The rising sophomore class was the best group of football prospects at Gloucester High in a decade. Forty-five kids were at the Lions football practice, and twenty were sophomores. The coaches had big expectations for the younger kids. Many of them were expected to earn starting positions this season. Fortunately for Oxley, there wasn't a standout running back in the group. There was a sophomore who was expected to step in at quarterback, a couple of fleet-footed wide receivers, and some weight room devotees who were expected to be two-way linemen.

After an hour of running drills and individual instruction, there was a mandatory water break. Some players quietly pondered the burden they were accepting by participating in football. Many of their friends were home playing video games or watching Netflix. A few players wondered whether they were up to the commitment. It was hot. There was no indication that this year's team was going to be any better than last year's. They thought about the benefits of working a paying job at an air-conditioned mall compared to the six-days-a-week grind of football. The coaches guided the players through their offensive plays. It was a positive way to ease into the new season. Everyone was attentive. The defensive coaches worked on the defensive alignments. A big challenge for coaches at small Group 1 schools is that the more skilled kids play both offense and defense. It was a challenge to prepare the same kids for alignments specifically developed for that week's opponent on both sides of the ball.

Oxley was running at halfback with the third team. He was anxious to see just how effective he could be but held back and went at a comfortable speed. He was familiar with the Lions' playbook and could have jogged through it blindfolded. The coaches devoted a good deal of time teaching the sophomores the nuanced plays that they may have only half-heartedly paid attention to as freshmen. No live hitting occurred except on the sleds, and the practice pace was brisk and efficient. The coaches remained enthused and encouraging as the first day of preparation for the 2016 season drew to a close. Coach Claiborn spoke before they headed to the locker room.

"Good first day. Real good first day. I like how the older guys were helping the sophomores. That's what leaders do—lead. The quicker the young guys master the plays and get comfortable with the offense and defense, the quicker we are going to be a formidable team. We appreciate how hard everyone is working. Keep your minds strong. You're going to be a bit sore and tired tomorrow when you wake up, but realize all of that quickly passes. We've all done this before. We're going to get better every day. The first week is tough but *we're* tough, right? If we weren't tough, we wouldn't be out here. Keep your minds strong. That's the key. Let's be dressed and ready and on the practice field at nine tomorrow."

The locker room was animated. The players felt this could be their year. They forgot they felt the same way after the first day of practice last year. The coaches were grounded in reality. The sophomores had talent and promise, but could they adjust to varsity competition? Will experienced veterans could become role models and leaders? Their kicker, an ex-soccer player who lacked the deft footwork required to excel on the soccer field, had gone to a kicking camp at Rowan University this summer and was probably the best kicker in the conference. He was also an adequate punter. They had reasons to be optimistic and reasons to be pessimistic, a coach's constant dilemma.

No one showered in the locker room, so it emptied out quickly as players hurried home to get cleaned up. Some of the seniors had cars and a couple offered Oxley a ride home. The boys kept their football equipment and practice jerseys in their lockers and walked through the parking lot in sweatpants, sweaty t-shirts, and sports sandals. Oxley accepted a ride home from Mike King, who lived down the street from him. They had been classmates since kindergarten. They talked about their summers and evaluated the football team's prospects moving forward. King was a returning starter at tight end and played some linebacker last season after injuries decimated the linebacker corps. He was expected to start both ways this season. He stood six feet tall and weighed two hundred pounds. He had good hands. The Lions threw to their tight end often last season because their wideouts were not very substantial. King was tough and dependable. His father was a plumber, so King planned to attend trade school after graduation to learn plumbing, too. He already knew a good deal about the trade from helping his dad each summer. He lacked the size and ambition to play college football. He respected the game and the coaches and felt proud to put on the blue and gold uniform each Friday night and represent his hometown on the gridiron.

"Get some rest, dude. Back at it again tomorrow," he said as he pulled in front of Oxley's house.

Oxley went inside and showered. He texted Barb to see if she wanted to get together after dinner.

"Don't you have to meet with Mandrake the Magician or whoever transformed you into Ezekiel Elliott?" she replied.

"You're hilarious."

"I'd love to hang out. Maybe we can play two-hand touch out back."

"Was I that bad last night?"

"You paid no attention at all to me, and I swear you looked in the mirror and flexed every time you walked past my dresser."

"I'm sorry. It was just a crazy day yesterday. So much stuff happened out of nowhere. It was crazy."

"If we actually told each other how we feel about each other, I'd say, 'Don't worry about it, dude. I still love you.' But since we don't, why don't you stop by after eating your dead animal sandwich at the pizzeria?"

"I've got protein requirements."

"I forgot that your muscles are suddenly the focal point of your life."

"I'm eating so much humble pie here that I might not even have an appetite for dinner. Was I that bad?"

"No. Sorry. Just upset that you didn't give me your undivided attention like you usually do, lol. It's usually the only attention I get, or maybe it's the only attention I want. I can't figure out which."

"Awkward silence on this end."

"I've decided to be more transparent about my feelings. At least via texting when I don't have to fret about your reaction immediately."

"I could be coy and not text back for a while."

"But you wouldn't because then you'd be like everyone else and you're not like everyone else."

"I'm just me."

"I found a diary I kept in junior high. Wait 'til I show you. Pretty hilarious. Poignant at times."

"Not many people write anything poignant in eighth grade, lol."

"Just text before you leave."

"I will."

"Later."

Barb found her current diary and made an entry commenting on her junior high musings:

Looking back on my diary from four years ago, I accept, however reluctantly, that I have grown. My guidance counselor is no longer my best friend. She is still one of my best friends but I no longer feel jealous when I see anyone else entering her office, as I apparently did back in junior high. I use to scan my mind for a "crisis" to discuss if I saw someone else walking down the hall with her or sitting in the junior high guidance office waiting area. Attention, attention, please, someone give me some attention! I can still detect that particular impulse in me. When I was in eighth grade, my mom started insisting I go to therapy. I remember how ashamed I felt that I was so flawed I actually needed professional assistance to keep myself together. I was resistant as can be to the idea. I discussed the idea with my counselor and she shared that she had been in therapy for years. She said entering therapy proves that we are strong enough to want to face ourselves. As soon as she said that, I felt the planet spin and I went home after school and started bugging my mom to make the appointment.

It makes me sad that not many people have understood me then or now. I've felt consistently lonely and ignored by people I hope notice me. I wanted to be a singer back then and it makes me wonder if all of the concentration on the piano demonstrates a loss of confidence in my singing or a realistic concentration on where my greater talent lies. I have a difficult time evaluating myself in so many facets of life. I'm only sure of these: I'm smart. I'm a quick study. I'm very sensitive but when hurt I become very insensitive to whoever hurt me. If you hurt me or disappoint me too many times, you become invisible to me. I'm resilient and wish I didn't have to continue being so resilient. I'm strong. Of these, I'm sure; everything else is in flux.

Back in junior high, I wrote that I wish I had a church to go to like some of my classmates. I still do. Or I wish I could find a spiritual path somehow. I read about different traditions and they sound either esoteric and unfathomable or too simplistic. I never feel grounded. My family structure has collapsed and offers no real support. The guidance staff offers support, but that will expire in nine months. If I find some sort of spiritual grounding, I might become more confident. I don't care what tradition I follow if it offers me solace and peace of mind. Maybe I'll try yoga and see where that leads.

In junior high, it looks like I was the only kid who didn't look forward to naps. I was and am a reluctant sleeper. My mind senses that I might miss out on something and fights unconsciousness. I haven't napped since I slept in a crib. My mind seeks stimulation, not annihilation. I can't even stay asleep at night.

Trust issues continue. Fear of vulnerability. Wondering what this life means and where it all leads. Grim evaluations of my physical appearance. I've morphed from complaining my boobs are too small to complaining they're too big. Yearning to be loved and understood. Yearning to be loved and understood. Yearning to be loved and understood. A common theme.

Oxley practiced the sax and walked to the pizzeria. He walked through the door and spotted McGrogan. He was sitting at the same booth as the night before and had the remnants of a small white pizza divided between his plate and the small aluminum pizza tray.

"I thought you were gone for a while?" Oxley asked.

"Needed to go over a few things with you so I had to stop back. Plus it's virtually the only place on earth to hear those great '60s masterpieces on a jukebox. And on analog vinyl, nonetheless. I'm thinking maybe you and that wack job are onto something."

"You're appreciating the sound of vinyl?"

"Humbly and belatedly, yes. By the way, are they wedding bells I'm hearing in the future for you and your fair maiden? I figured two were just a future cabaret act at the Algonquin. Once again, I'm humbled."

Oxley felt a sharp sting at the top of his ear. He turned and saw Ray Thones and two other self-styled badasses walk by. Thones turned his head on the way to the pizza counter to enjoy Oxley's discomfort.

"Worse friggin' football player in history. Think he plays the tuba in the marching band but still come out for football every year. What a wuss," Thones told his friends.

"One of your football pals?" McGrogan asked.

"He's unbearable," Oxley replied.

"Are you guys ever on opposite sides of the ball at practice?"

"Frequently."

"Well, sonny, I'm not telling you what to do but let me make a little suggestion. When you finally unleash the beast, make sure that caveman's in the immediate vicinity. Run his ass over every chance you get, and then lay low again for a while."

"I only see the guy at football. He's obnoxious."

Thones had picked up his pizza and walked by on the way out, waving his wrist limply at Oxley.

"Bye bye, band boy," Thones said, affecting as feminine a voice as his limited imagination allowed.

"I'd love to beat his ass myself," McGrogan said, "but I won't steal that pleasure from you."

"What else do you need a tell me?" Oxley asked, trying to ignore the indignity.

"Well, you're a smart kid so not a whole heckuva lot. What I do have to tell you is essential. No mention of any of this hocus pocus to anybody but the love that dares not speak its name, Barbara."

"How do you know all of this stuff that happens in private? It's striking me as somewhere between alarming and scary."

"If I had to put a wager down, I'd bet on scary. For now, play it smart at practice. Play it low key. Try to blend in for a while. There will be plenty of time to stand out. You're used to blending in. You're good at it. Flex your muscles once in a while to get somebody's attention. It's all kind of meaningless until the real season begins. But if you find yourself isolated at any time with that jackass that just came in here, teach him to respect you. Run him over a few times. Don't even break stride. Run right through him. With any luck, he'll bite off part of his tongue or something."

"That's it?"

"Yeah that's it. I wanted to make sure that LuLuBelle is the only person you're speaking to about any of this. You jolted me a bit last night. I'd figured you were the strong silent type. Never figured you guys were secretly in love and you'd want to share your feelings with her. It can only bear a certain amount of scrutiny. Loose lips sink ships and all that."

"Gotcha."

"You're on your own for a while, amigo. I will get in touch if I need to get in touch."

"See you."

McGrogan walked out the door and Nick's sister-in-law, Angie, started to walk over to Oxley with his sandwich.

"I'll come over to the counter like usual. Sorry."

"Who was that guy? He's got a weird vibe."

"He's a football trainer. He's not going to be around very often."

"There's too many hanger-ons with that football program. People need to let you kids be kids."

Oxley knocked on Barb's front door lightly and walked in. Barb wore a Slayer t-shirt that had been washed and worn so many times it had become nearly transparent. She was practicing the piano. Barb's mom and grandmom had both played and the piano had been in her family forever. It was a Wing & Son Style 29 upright piano made of mahogany. The piano must have been a hundred years old and still sounded great. Barb played Horace Silver's "Song for My Father." Oxley stood behind her so he could watch her fingers dance over the piano keys. He remained silent for a few seconds after she finished and said, "You are amazing. Maybe you should just play solo piano up at Rutgers. You're talented. You're really going to be a professional musician some day."

"So are you, Oxley. You're super talented. Your playing is soulful as anything. You risk being vulnerable when you play. Maybe you should try to access that place more in your daily life."

Oxley ignored her.

"Your piano playing is sublime," he said.

"I practice so much, it better sound good. I get by on technique, I'm afraid. I want more of what you have. To not be so self-conscious when I'm playing. I dislike feeling like there's a spotlight on me. I hardly ever feel that way in real life. I don't care a bit what most people think of me. But when I'm at the piano, the spotlight becomes too focused."

"I feel the opposite almost. I think everyone's judging me and ready to criticize me in my daily life but I forget myself when I play."

She got up from the piano bench.

"I'm hungry. Want some grapes?"

"No, thanks. I went to Joe's."

"Something different! They should name a sandwich after you. Maybe when you're a famous jazz musician."

"Is there such a thing as a famous jazz musician?"

They sat down at Barb's kitchen table while she ate the bowl of grapes. Barb was a vegetarian but ate cookies, cupcakes, candy, and french fries. Oxley ate meat but avoided anything with sugar. They had argued the merits of each diet for so long that they lost interest in the topic.

"Guess who was at Joe's?"

"Not that spooky guy? C'mon, Oxley. You should Google him. He's probably on the Megan's Law list."

"I did Google him. There's no mention of him anywhere."

"Why is he interested in you? Why not some hotshot athlete somewhere?"

"I don't know, man. It's very strange."

"Did you finish your Anatomy packet? It's due the first day of classes."

"I had football all day. Physicals, equipment pick up, practice. I didn't have time for anything."

"Ever notice that we lose our momentum as soon as football starts every year? We stop playing music together for a while. You start depending on me to complete the summer assignments."

"Yeah. Sorry. I don't have the time. I'll wake up tomorrow feeling sore all over. It even hurts to sleep the first few days. Pain and discomfort are big disincentives from doing anything."

"I wish you'd just drop football. It subtracts something from you."

"But it adds something to me, too."

"Right."

"Do you want to do some of the Anatomy now?"

"I worked on it for a few hours this afternoon when you were out playing with that thug Thones and your other buddies."

"Can I take it home later and copy it? It's a joint project."

"Dude, you make me want to smoke a joint. Yes, you can have it. Let's go listen to some music."

They went to Barb's room and she put a record from a '60s British prog rock band Audience on the turntable. They sat on the floor alongside her bed. Oxley closed his eyes and tried to relax. Barb folded her arms and continued to fume. She got up and turned the volume down on her receiver. Oxley opened his eyes.

"What's the matter?"

"Oxley, I want to be more than just than just friends. I have feelings for you, and I'm tired of trying to ignore them or suppress them. I'm frustrated."

"Can you be more specific?"

"Can you be less of a douchebag? You realize there's a strong connection between us that transcends the music, transcends the fact that we are fellow outcasts, that we have similar quirky tastes, that we can relax around each other. You think it, but do you feel it?"

"I have the same feelings for you."

"Have you ever contemplated *acting* on those feelings?"

"I never know what to do. It feels like my mind is in one spot, my soul's in another, and my body's in another. I don't know how to connect them so I just stay in my mind. It's the only part of me I can trust."

"That's driving with the brakes on. There's a bunch of energy you're keeping clamped off."

"Just bear with me. I'm glad we're talking about it. I'm unconscious too much of the time. Reality bugs me, so I retreat."

"I don't want to just be pals with you, Oxley. We're like seventh graders instead of seventeen-year-olds. And, of course, I'm going to bear with you. I want this stuff out in the open though. I have strong, positive feels for someone whose default setting is full retreat. Let's at least meet in the middle somewhere. I'll be patient with you but I feel like I have been patient for a long while now. I'm running out of patience."

The football team practiced in the mornings for the remainder of the summer. Practice lasted three hours. Every player had to participate in six practices before they could participate in a scrimmage against another school. The first scrimmage was scheduled against Palmyra. Until then, intrasquad scrimmages were permitted. Most of the players arrived at 8:00 to get dressed, see the school's athletic trainer, hydrate, and get out to the practice field by 9 a.m. The locker room was subdued. Many players had been asleep at this hour since school let out in June. Their bodies were adjusting to the new schedule. The players acknowledged their friends with head nods or a few words. Only Thones was raucous at this hour:

"Live contact starts today, girls. Hopefully I hit a few of you hard enough that you don't come back."

He wasn't taken seriously enough for anyone to respond but he did make people uneasy. Coach Claiborn started practice by reminding the players what it has meant over the years to wear the blue and gold Lions football jersey.

"It's an honor and an obligation," he said.

The players ran through drills for the first hour and then offense and defense separated for individual instruction.

Anyone who played both offense and defense switched after thirty minutes. Oxley played halfback for the offense after the two players ahead of him on the depth chart switched to defense. He could hear Thones' loud mouth echoing from the defensive side of the field.

"Better hope you two never get hurt. Imagine having a marching band fairy at halfback."

The final hour of practice was devoted to live scrimmaging. Oxley watched form the sidelines for a while but was inserted with the first team after two-way starters were moved from offense to defense. He'd be running the football for the first time in a scrimmage since he'd met McGrogan. He ran at half speed for a while until he adjusted to his new powers. He was used as a blocker for the first five plays, then the coaches called his number. He followed his fullback through a hole and picked up 3 yards before being wrapped up by two linebackers. The coaches called his number again the following play. It was designed to go through the same hole, but the defensive linemen had pushed through this time so Oxley decided to run to the outside, a move he wouldn't have tried in the past. Mike King had blocked the defensive end and Oxley saw daylight, ran around the right end, and headed down the sideline. The defensive back was approaching him head on so he cut back toward the center of the field and saw Thones bearing down on him at full speed. At the last second, Oxley feinted left for a moment, pulled back, and spun. Thones ended up diving full speed at his ankles but missed and went sliding along the field. Oxley was tackled by two defenders after a gain of 10 yards, but his teammates were hollering and celebrating the fact that Thones had missed him.

"Nice tackle."

"What were you saying about the band kid?"

Thones was furious.

"You see what he did? He spun backwards rather than get tackled. Just wait until next time."

"Nice run," Coach Claiborn said. "Let's run the same play but let's get off the blocks better. The only guy who held his block that time was Kingy. We need some O-line pride. C'mon!"

The play developed differently and the offensive line pushed the defensive line backwards. Oxley followed his full-back to the gap behind the right guard. He ran through the hole and decided it was time to flex his muscles. Thones was coming at him full speed. Oxley accelerated. He plowed into Thones in full stride, lifting his shoulder at the last moment to initiate contact. Thones was thrown back three feet and Oxley sprinted 40 yards into the end zone without anyone else laying a hand on him. There was complete silence on the field. Mike King was the first to speak.

"What the heck just happened?"

The players laughed and jogged to meet Oxley walking back from the end zone.

"Dude, what was that?"

"That was awesome, man!"

Kids who never spoke to Oxley were patting him on the back and congratulating him. Coach Claiborn was grinning.

"Who was that guy?" he asked. "Nice burst of speed, John."

The teams went back to their huddles. Thones was on the sidelines being assisted by the trainer. There were fifteen minutes left to practice and Oxley laid back and blended in again. His run lifted everyone's spirits and when Coach Claiborn spoke at the end of practice, he mentioned that Oxley showed up every day for three years, learned the plays, never complained about a lack of playing time, never saw playing for the JVs as a demotion or beneath him, and now maybe was about to come into his own.

The locker room mood was celebratory. Players were thinking that if a guy like Oxley could show major improvement, there was no telling how good some of the more talented players could be. They were happy that a quiet guy like Oxley might become a contributor, as improbable as that seemed until an hour ago. Thones never came out to another day of football.

Oxley was a marginal talent the first three seasons and always felt he was viewing things from the periphery. Now he was part of the team's core. He continued to show bursts of potential. The coaches were supportive and encouraging. Every player was treated equally and the coaches treated Oxley as they always had. Gloucester played Palmyra in their opening scrimmage. The scrimmage was more useful for gauging whether players had mastered the intricacies of the offense and defense than as a barometer of the team's strength. Oxley carried the ball five times and gained 28 yards. That would have qualified for an unqualified success last season, so he continued to get the coaches' attention as a player who was ready to contribute this season.

The remainder of the preseason went smoothly. Oxley remained the third option at halfback and continued to pull his punches when he carried the ball. He was curious about how effective he could be if he went full speed, but the regular season began on the first Friday of the school year so he would find out soon. He hadn't heard from McGrogan. He continued to lift at the PAL Club in the afternoons and knew his strength had greatly increased. Word of his success on the football team filtered back to the police officers who monitored the PAL, and they were supportive and happy that Oxley was going to be a varsity contributor. They saw how much stronger he was. Right before Labor Day weekend, Oxley asked Officer Mike Morrow to spot him so he could max out before cutting back the volume of lifting when school began on Tuesday. The football coaches had a maintenance program during Monday practices and that would be all the lifting Oxley would do each week. Morrow spotted him, and Oxley maxed out on the bench at 285 pounds.

"Buddy, that is crazy! I've only seen one person add over a hundred pounds to their bench strength in less than a year—and that was with sustained training with a strength coach, a perfect diet for adding muscle, vitamins, supplements, and probably a few things I didn't know about. You've gone up over a hundred pounds over the course of the summer, something I'd swear was impossible."

"I'm as amazed as you."

"Don't take offense, John, but you're not taking steroids or HGH or anything, right? Your body definition changed a lot over the past few months. You're not working with one of those Russian Olympic weightlifting coaches or anything, right?"

The joke cut the tension and Oxley assured him he wouldn't know how to get any of the illegal supplements even if he wanted them.

"There are guys in every weight room who know how to get them, even high school weight rooms. Unfortunately, it's part of weight room culture."

"I only lift here. And even if someone on the team thought that was the way to go, he sure wouldn't have told me about it. They looked at me more like I was one of the managers than one of the players. I only started getting their respect as an athlete in the last two weeks. I'm clean. It's just a fluke. Maybe I had latent potential."

"Some university physiology and human potential professors would love to study you, buddy. It's freakish. But it couldn't have happened to a better kid. I'm happy for you. Best of luck this season. We'll be coming to the games."

"Thanks for everything. Thanks for taking the time to help me in here. I always appreciate it." They shook hands and Oxley walked down Brown Street to his house.

He showered, cobbled together some of his mother's leftovers for lunch, and practiced the sax. At this point, Oxley was fully committed to attending Rutgers as a music major. He would suggest to Barb that they play two Stan Getz pieces for his Rutgers audition. With football, he wouldn't have time to master the intricacies of the Jackie McLean pieces. Stan Getz played a more straightforward style that was easier to learn and practice. Oxley was practicing two songs that Getz performed at the end of his career: "Sunshower" and "Joanne Julia." Two potential benefits of switching to the Getz songs were that Getz played with Kenny Barron, Barb's favorite pianist, and that with any luck, Barron might be present for their audition; he was a distinguished music professor at Rutgers and had written both numbers.

Barb practiced the role of Dotty in the Gloucester High drama club production of *Noises Off* each afternoon for performances the final weekend of September. As a consequence, Oxley saw less of Barb and had time to reflect on the direction of their relationship. As Barb said, they might be the first couple to break up without ever having gone out.

Oxley's mom worked for a division of Holt Logistics that imported fruit from Chile and distributed it to supermarkets and grocers throughout the Philadelphia region. She inspected fruit vessels and refrigerated warehouses and enforced FDA rules and regulations for ready-to-eat human food. She searched for any sign of food contamination and maintained spotless warehouses where the fruit was stored. She implemented Safe Operating Procedures as specified by the Food Safety Modernization Act. Eating, drinking, and smoking was forbidden in any warehouse storing fruit, and Oxley's mom enforced this regulation stringently. She took her position seriously and felt responsibility to both her on-site customers—the market owners—and her off-site customers—the Chilean farmers. Oxley's mom flew to Chile three times a year to maintain relationships with the farm collectives. She proudly displayed her audit scores, ninety-six percent for 2014 and ninety-nine percent for 2015, on the refrigerator in Oxley's kitchen.

"No other port facility on the East Coast has accomplished scores this high on safe quality for certifications," she assured Oxley.

Because of her continuing success in maintaining the food safety program for DelMonte, Oxley's mother had gained one promotion after another, and now managed a food safety team selected from each division of the company. She worked with Hershey, Primus, and DelMonte, as well as governmental safety regulators such as OSHA and the Food and Drug Administration. She traveled to other company affiliates on the East Coast. With each success, she was home less and less. Oxley and his mother maintained a level of trust uncommon during a typical adolescence. He was proud of how much she had accomplished, moving into lower management of a multimillion dollar company without a college diploma, and realized her absences were driven more by economic necessity rather than personal ambition.

The 2016-2017 school year opened the Tuesday after Labor Day. The excitement of being reunited with their friends mingled with the shock students' bodies felt about being wide awake at 8 a.m. after a summer of sleeping until noon. Kids who stayed up late playing video games all summer found the habit impossible to stop now that school was opening. Homeroom started at 8:10. The soccer, field hockey, cross country, and football teams were prepared to open their season this week. The fall sports pep rally was scheduled for Friday. Announcements were made about fundraisers that would be held throughout the fall to help defray the cost of the senior class trip to Disney World in March. A few students had moved away and new kids appeared in the hallways. Some veteran teachers had retired, and some new faces were in the front of the classrooms as well. The week's lunch menus were posted. Teachers delighted in seeing certain colleagues and dreaded seeing others. Administrators greeted the students as they entered. A new school year was about to begin.

Oxley had a grueling academic schedule: AP Literature and Composition, AP Psychology, AP Anatomy and Physiology,

Calculus, AP U.S. History, and Music Theory. Barb had Oxley's academic classes minus the history class, plus Design and Illustration, and choir during her lunch period. Because of her commitment to the school choir, Oxley and Barb didn't sit together at lunch for the first time since seventh grade. He had sixth period lunch and sat on the periphery of the two tables where the senior football players ate. He listened to their conversations and was startled when he looked across the table and saw a girl he had never seen before standing behind the seat directly across from him.

"Is anyone sitting here? I'm new and I don't know anyone."

Oxley awkwardly motioned for her to sit down and within a millisecond, every eye at the table bulged in her direction. She had long dark hair, a beautiful smile, a flawless complexion, and she was blushing. She wore Eve Denim high-waisted Charlotte culottes and a Meek Mill t-shirt.

"I moved here a couple of days ago from Florida. I just registered for school Friday. My name's Devan DeBree."

"I'm Oxley. My first name's John but everyone calls me by my last name."

There was a chorus of other voices offering introductions but Devan seemed content to converse with Oxley.

"Are you a senior?" he asked.

"I'm a junior, but the only lunch period they could squeeze me in was this one. New Jersey has certain graduation requirements that Florida doesn't have and vice versa, so my schedule's a mixture of classes that Florida didn't require but New Jersey does and normal junior-year classes. I'm fine with the schedule. School comes easily to me even though I can't say I like it much."

"What brought you to New Jersey?"

"My mom and her boyfriend were splitting up, and she wanted to get as far away from him as she could. A friend had visited Gloucester City a few times and spoke highly of the place. Said it had a nice retro '60s vibe. Small town, USA, and all that."

"I think you'll like it. The school has a good atmosphere. It's supportive and friendly. The town's pretty laid back. People look out for each other."

"What do you do for excitement?"

"I like music a lot. I play the sax in the concert band."

"Wow! I'm having lunch with a musician."

"That's what I hope to do for a living, become a professional musician."

"Can you really make a living doing that anymore? I can see gambling on it if you had an indie band or rapped, but a sax player? I don't know. Is that really a viable career these days?"

"I sure hope so. But I guess I'm not sure. I also play football for the high school. Our first game is Friday."

"That's exciting. Do a lot of people come to the games?"

"Yeah, the town is pretty crazy about sports. It's like their main focus."

"It's cool that you're going to be a part of it. Is the game home or away?"

"The opener is away at Clayton."

"Is Clayton far from here? I have a car. Maybe I'll take a drive down."

"That would be great. I hope we have a good season. I think we will."

"Can't wait to see you play. My mom's boyfriend was a big Miami Dolphins fan. Lots of Dan Marino memorabilia around the basement."

"Can't say I ever heard of him."

"Old-time Dolphins great. I heard you're pretty darn good yourself."

"Whoever told you that is being kind. Those guys at the other table are good. You should talk to them."

"I'll be looking forward to the game on Friday. Someone told me you're on the verge of a breakout season. That's exciting. A nice kid who is finally coming into his own. That's what people are saying."

"People are really saying stuff like that?'

"People in the know are."

Devan said goodbye and the moment as she was out of earshot, Oxley's teammates were tousling his hair and teasing him.

"Who is she?"

"I want your life, Oxley. Damn, dude."

He didn't give another thought to Devan the rest of the school day. Football practice went well. Nagging injuries had kept certain players out the first few weeks of practices, but the good showing in their scrimmages motivated some players to get back into action. Mike King had been driving Oxley home after practice every day, but when the players came out of the locker room, Devan walked out the school exit near the cafeteria doors and casually strolled across the parking lot to her car, a 2016 Volkswagen Jetta Sport painted a metallic cardinal red. She spotted Oxley and yelled, "Hey Oxley, do you need a ride?"

Oxley began to say that he was riding home with Mike, but King elbowed him in the ribs and whispered,

"Are you kidding, dude? Get over there now."

Oxley shrugged and walked over to Devan. He hadn't showered and was dirty and sweaty from practice.

"Sure you want me in your car? I'm a bit dusty."

"Get in, will you?"

She had a Fender eight-speaker sound system and blared *Coloring Book* by Chance the Rapper so loudly that conversation was impossible. After they pulled out of the high school parking lot, she turned down the volume.

"Where do you live anyway?"

"North Brown Street."

"You'll have to direct me, John. I don't know any of the streets yet."

"Go down Greenwood to the very end and turn left. It's not that far. Thanks for the ride. Why were you at school so late?"

"I forgot my laptop in my locker so I had to come back. I have homework already."

"Left on Highland, then drive by the lakes and the ballfields to the blinking light at Hudson."

"Wanna help me with my homework? I heard you're a brainiac."

"Uh, I have to shower, eat, practice my sax, and do my own homework. Some other night might be better, if you're ever really stuck. Here's my house."

"All right, John. Is there a girlfriend in the picture? I don't want to stir anything up."

"I'm not sure."

"You're not sure if you have a girlfriend?" She laughed. "Most people are pretty sure one way or the other."

"It's complicated."

"They're all complicated. If you had to answer absolutely 'yes' or absolutely 'no,' what would the answer be?"

"Probably 'no.'"

"Yay! So I might have a chance!"

"Eh, I'll see you tomorrow. Hope your homework's not too tough."

Oxley got out and headed into the house. Within seconds, his phone buzzed. It was a text from Barb.

"Dude, are you kidding me! That Kardashian wannabe vampire chick drove you home from practice??"

"We literally just pulled up and you know already?"

"Dude, it's Gloucester. Everybody knows everything. Did you think no one was going to see you?"

"It was innocent as anything. She was coming out of the school just as we got out of practice."

"Did Mike King's car break down? Why didn't you just ride home with him like every other night?"

"I don't know, Barb. She was just there so I took the ride."

"It seems calculated as hell that she would be there three hours after school got out at the exact moment you guys came out of the locker room. I heard she had a boner for you at lunch today."

"Why are you making a big deal of it?"

"Grrrrrrrrrrrrrrrrrrrrrrr."

When Oxley tried to text her back, his number was blocked.

Devan DeBree, formerly Renee Bauman, formerly Debbie Klein, formerly Cherie Rommelman, formerly Kristin Underwood, and formerly Danielle Bond, was born and raised in Asheville, North Carolina. The name on her birth certificate read Danielle Bond.

One Friday evening in June, just after she had graduated from Asheville High School, Devan was standing along the periphery of a drum circle in Pritchard Park on Patton Avenue. Hundreds of people were in the park beating hand drums, bongos, cowbells, triangles, and other percussive instruments. Other people danced, some with hula hoops around their waists. Many people felt energized by the drum circle and whirled around for hours each Friday. Devan stood at College Street and watched, bobbing her head gently. She had mousy brown hair, brown eyes, and a soft down along her jawline, which obscured her facial contours. Her hair was thinning. She had an overbite that couldn't be corrected without surgery to her jaw. She was not unattractive but you had to use your imagination to see the beauty hidden in her looks. Her aunt once asked her if she had broken her nose because of the distinct ridge that appeared a few inches from her eyes. She had slumped shoulders, wore glasses, and had a doughy complexion from eating a diet heavy in carbs and low in fruits and veggies. She held a pair of roller skates with the laces tied together.

"Ever get tired of being on the outside looking in?" a man asked, ruddy faced and with fine white hair. He wore a tie-dyed t-shirt that read "Beats Me."

"Do I know you?" Devan asked.

"Not yet. We're just meeting. Ponder that question: aren't you tired of being on the outside looking in? Like everyone else is experiencing the song and dance but you're standing on the periphery, watching, wondering where's your share of the joy?"

"It's crossed my mind. I think it crosses everyone's mind."

"I don't think it's crossing anyone's mind who is over there dancing or making music. They're having fun. You're watching."

"I've always been a wallflower."

"Doesn't look like a whole lotta fun."

"What's it to you, anyway?"

"I might just be the person to jump start your life. I'd say it's a very fortuitous meeting. I think if you adhere to a program I've developed, you'll be turning heads everywhere you walk. You'll be an object of desire and not an object of people's sympathy."

"What kind of program, like a cult?"

"Nahhh. Nothing crazy. No real commitment either. I make a slight adjustment similar to a chiropractor, we get you a little augmentation to smooth out the rough edges, and voila! Every dream you ever dreamed is suddenly possible."

"I really don't have much time for any program. I'm going to be applying for jobs starting tomorrow. I just graduated high school. Some of my friends are over in the park, dancing and goofing around."

"I don't care what kind of job you are interviewing for—looking like you belong in Hollywood never hurts."

"What's the catch?"

"The devil's always in the details, isn't it, honey? How about we meet for lunch tomorrow at Tupelo Honey in downtown Asheville? It's a public place. You can get up and walk out if I say anything the slightest bit offensive. Hear what I have to say. If you're interested, I'll be there at noon."

"I'll think about it. What's your name, again?"

"The name's McGrogan, Bill McGrogan. Here's my card."

The card read: *Fly By Night Enterprises and Wounded Dragon Special Effects. Be the change you wish to see in the world.*

"The card doesn't have a phone number or web page."

"I don't need them. I do all my business in person."

Devan hung out along College Street until her friends got tired of dancing and fooling around. She was feeling less and less a part of her core group of high school friends. Most of them were excited about getting ready for college, some heading to Chapel Hill, some heading to Raleigh Durham, some getting ready for UNC Asheville. Devan was unenthusiastic about attending college. High school had been painful and boring. Moving to Orlando and trying to get an entry level job at Disney sounded more exciting. She had friends who were working the concessions at Universal.

The following morning, she got dressed, showered, and caught the NextBus to downtown Asheville. She walked to the Tupelo Honey Cafe on College Street and waited to hear what McGrogan could offer. McGrogan arrived a few minutes later, his face sunburned and his fine white hair waving slightly from the conveyor belt ceiling fans in the restaurant. They both ordered sweet potato pancakes with peach butter and admired the wall art by local folk artists.

"All right, what's the deal exactly, Mr. McGrogan? I may not be the best student around but that's a matter of interest, not ability. I'm as smart as anyone else. I'm just not enthused about the stuff they teach in classrooms. Don't think you're dealing with some Southern bunny. Make sense to me."

"I'm not sure what I say will make sense but I am sure that what I say will improve your life immensely. More dreams will come true in a single afternoon than in a month of Sundays."

"So what's the deal?"

"I deal in dream magic. Dreams that people don't dare to admit to even their very best friends. I have a way to make those dreams come true."

"And how do you do that?"

"I'm a Karma Cleaner. You would have a difficult time watching a movie nowadays, reading a magazine, or even talking with friends where the concept of 'karma' doesn't come up. It's become an accepted fact of life, am I right?"

"Karma? Yes, heard about it, talked about it, thought about it. Karma Cleaner? First time I've ever heard that concept."

"Believing in the time-honored concept of karma is a good place to begin. A common ground, if you will. Keep an open mind, and I'll elaborate on further truths about the concept. Violence and drugs like cocaine and heroin are damaging to anyone's karma. With me so far?"

"I'm with you."

"I have a client down in Miami Beach. She's a female who sings in a nightclub owned by her father. She's used massive amounts of powdered cocaine for months and months and months and gotten herself into a jam. Wouldn't hear of entering a rehab facility, no matter who begged her. Out of control in every phase of her life. A week ago, she stuck a steak knife in her boyfriend's rib cage. Now she's waving a white flag from her jail cell, she wants to go to rehab. From where she's sitting now, a drug rehab in southern California looks inviting, like a hacienda even."

"What's all this got to do with me?"

"You have great karma. I'm not casting aspersions on your life so far, but it's pretty plain vanilla. You're kind. Intelligent. Thoughtful. Compassionate. Friend to animals. And she's none of these."

"So?"

"So when she goes in front of a judge, if she has to lug around her bad karma, let's just say it's off-putting and unpleasant. She's a royal bitch who kicks little dogs, laughs at homeless people as she whizzes by in her Land Rover, and sticks a knife in her boyfriend. Not much to recommend. Any judge trying to 'get a feel for her' will be instantly repulsed. I would like to switch your karma for her karma. It won't change anything in terms of your experience and satisfaction of life. You, just by being you, will begin to instantly modify her bad karma. In a little while, you'll be completely balanced again. In return, I will transform you into the best-looking girl in North Carolina, which is saying something. It'd be a lot easier for me to promise than if we were in, say, Maine. But North Carolina sets the bar very high for beauty, and you're about to soar over that bar, if you'd like."

"Will I be a singer?"

"No. I never said she's a singer. I said she sings in her family's club. She can't sing for shit."

"And I stay completely me but am transformed into a rare beauty?"

"Yes, ma'am. The rarest in the land, if I may be so bold."

"Does it involve an operation?"

"It does not. Have you heard of pop-up shops?"

"Like for jeans and clothing?"

"Exactly. Only this is a pop-up for ageless beauty. When you leave here, walk down to Haywood Street. Are you familiar with the great Malaprop's Bookstore?"

"Been there many times."

"Perfect. Walk past the store and you will see a hand-painted sign advertising Fly By Night Beauty Culture, a division of Fly By Night Enterprises, of which I am the humble proprietor. Have you heard of one-day-only sales at the mall? Most of them are a complete scam. Not us. The shop won't even be here tomorrow. It leaves when you leave, that's my motto."

"And what will happen if I go to the shop?"

"We offer a full range of beauty upgrades: lower-eyelid blepharoplasty to reposition fat under the eyes. Injectable filler between the earlobe and jawbone. Thermal radiofrequency skin tightening. Neck cord Botox injections. New hair color and new hair. Botox temple of the dog injections. Laser skin resurfacing. Takes about five minutes and you're not 'as good as new,' you *are* new. Prettier than you've ever imagined. And we offer a brand new pair of roller skates with each service, in case you want to trip the light fantastic at the big drum circle next Friday."

"Think I'll pass on the roller skates."

"Please promise me you're not going to watch everyone else have fun again even with your Ava Gardner beauty upgrade! You'd hurt my feelings."

"So I become beautiful, she goes to rehab, then what?"

"You will sign a contract, legally binding in three solar systems, stating that after one hundred days, you can reclaim your rather pedestrian looks, or decide to keep the Ava Gardner upgrade. Entirely up to you, dear. No strings attached."

"And if I keep the beauty upgrade?"

"Hollywood's a possibility. A spot on *The Bachelor*. Voice lessons perhaps, if you insist on becoming a singer. The wheel's still in spin, and there's no telling who it's naming."

"How long do I have to think it over?"

"Until I scoop the last bit of nutmeg off this plate with my finger. You have nothing to lose, dear. You'll receive a beauty treatment that will shock even your closest friends. I would wager not many people have been jealous of you up to this point. You will be a jealousy lightning rod by mid-afternoon, I promise. Or my name's not Bill McGrogan."

"And I can walk right over to Haywood Street and look for your sign?"

"Darling, I'd do it right here, but I don't think anybody wants dermabrasion residue in their peach butter, do you? First, I have to make slight adjustment to your lower sternum. The human sternum is shaped like a neck tie and there's an important point down the very bottom called the xiphoid process. I will touch it lightly with my thumb and three fingers. I make that adjustment, all of the changes in the beauty shop will become permanent, if you'd like. It's noninvasive and not anywhere you'd wear a bathing suit. We can do it on a street corner, if you prefer."

"Be my guest."

McGrogan leaned across the table and tweaked her lower sternum.

"All done. You're ready for the magic. You in?"

"I'm in. Do I get to see you afterward in case I have questions or concerns?"

"You know me, I'm directed in life by my stomach. What do you say we meet for an early dinner at the Sunny Point Cafe on Haywood? Four o'clock? Let's dine al fresco. The weather around here is perfect. I'll reserve us a table and we can celebrate with some shrimp and grits."

"Can't believe I'm about to do this," she giggled.

"Remember the null set in math? That's how many people have ever asked me for their old looks back. Christmas is coming early for you, honeybunch."

Devan walked down Haywood past Malaprop's Bookstore and sure enough, she saw a hand-painted sign that stated:

Fly By Night Beauty Culture. By appointment only. Hours 1:10-1:15 p.m. Saturdays only.

Devan walked through a curtained entrance, smelled ether, and sat down quickly in a chair like the one in the barber shop where her father used to take her as a child. She woke from a slumber sitting at a table in the cafe at Malaprop's. The table in front of her was littered with children's books, and a woman holding a child on her lap said, "Honey, you still have some hair dye or something on your forehead. Why don't you go check the mirror in the ladies room?"

Devan got up, shook her head a few times to fight the drowsiness, and walked to the bathroom. She gripped the sink with both hands and focused her eyes upon the mirror. The transition was startling. Her hair was a thick and lustrous jet black. Her eyes twinkled a greenish blue in the overlit bathroom. Her teeth were straight and gleamed a bright white in the mirror. Her nose was pert and flawless, her posture erect, her tummy firm, her skin bronze and blemish free. Her vision was clear and distinct. Devan stared for ten minutes, turning to view her features in silhouette, then wet a paper towel to erase the dye residue from her upper forehead. She couldn't tell if she was dreaming. She left the lavatory, walked through the bookstore, and out into the blazing June sunshine. It took a moment to regain her sense of direction, then she spun and walked to the Sunny Point Cafe to meet McGrogan.

"Hope you don't mind me saying so, but I'm looking at the prettiest young lady in the Great Smoky Mountains. What a transition! What do you think?"

"Amazing! What do I tell people when I see them? My family? My friends?"

"I know what I'd tell them, but that's just me. Tell them you found a salon you liked but they went out of business after you left."

"No, really. What do I say? The transformation is startling to me. I can't imagine what other people are going to think or say."

"Who cares what they think? Who cares what they say? If they don't like it, find some new friends. And that brings me to part two of our little bargain."

"Uh oh."

"Uh oh, nothing. It's all good, sugar. I forgot to tell you that this deal comes with free travel and liberal allowances for rent and furniture. I saw a chair you might like in New York last week. Do you like Italian Modernism? It was a real beauty by Marco Zanuso. And it's pink. My intuition tells me you'd like it. How much is your furniture allowance? How about unlimited? How's that sound?"

"Everything seems too good to be true."

"You hungry? I heard the rhubarb vinaigrette is amazing. You like salads?"

"I feel a bit woozy. Not really hungry. I'll sit and talk, though."

"In that case, darling, it's time to fly the coop. I got rock star trouble in Monaco. Karma Cleaners are hard to find. I will be back in touch at some point. Here's a credit card for you. It's my company card, Fly By Night Enterprises. Tax breaks and all that. But before I go, how about giving me your John Hancock on this one hundred-day contract. You get the Ava Gardner upgrade, unlimited rent and furniture allowance.... Would you like a line of credit at Malaprop's? If you're not going to college, might help to keep up with your reading."

"I'm good, thanks. How's the singer, have you heard?"

"How's the nut job is more like it. She's not much of a singer. But thanks for asking. She's fine. Sounded delighted to acquire the karma upgrade. Had all the warmth of a rattlesnake before we made the switch. Goes in front of the judge tomorrow. If she appears angelic enough, he might send her to a rehab. Ahh, here's a pen. Thank you for signing. No one's ever regretted doing business with me. Just a long line of satisfied clients. And good luck with the nosy neighbors or whoever you're worried about not liking the brand new you."

"Can I use the credit card to get out of here?"

"Out of Asheville?"

"It's just going to be too crazy explaining how I've transformed from Plain Jane to a Kardashian lookalike."

"Now that you mentioned it, I do see a certain resemblance."

"My friends are leaving for college soon. People are moving away. I've got nothing to hold me here. I can stay in touch with my family through the phone and computer."

"Like everybody else does nowadays. It's the brand new you. Where do you think you'd like to go? Flight By Night Enterprises has opportunities in all fifty states and the District of Columbia. You'll be part of a growing company with lots of opportunities for advancement. All relocation expenses will be picked up by the company, of course. And all of those hula hoopers and hippies will get along just fine without you."

"What kind of jobs would be available?"

"I see you being indispensable in managing assets."

"Financial assets? I can barely keep the minimum amount in my checking."

"Human assets. You have good people skills. Let's put them to good use. With your new exterior, fellas might find you mesmerizing."

"Any suggestions where the best opportunities are?"

"We have a phenomenal opportunity at present out in Bend, Oregon. Every been to Bend? I like the sound of that. Indulge me for a minute. Ever been to Bend? Ever been to Bend?"

McGrogan rehearsed it with varying accents.

"Ever been to Bend, darling?"

"No. I've never been to Bend," she said, giggling.

"Ever been to the great Pacific Northwest?"

"I've spent my entire life so far in either Asheville or Jacksonville, Florida."

"Home of the Jacksonville Jaguars!"

"I was little when we lived there."

"Think you're up for trying Bend? It's a truly great city. I'd suggest immediately getting into the whole fitness scene.

Bend is a town that appreciates human potential and tweaking the body toward optimal performance. Yoga studios galore, maybe a dozen bicycle shops, jogging trails along rivers, hiking trails up and down mountains, kayaking, body building, Pilates, hot yoga, outdoor yoga, mountain yoga, skiing. I've seen people in Bend spend three or four hours a day on a bicycle, I'm talking every day. Every single day."

"I'd like to give it a try."

"Now the one thing I don't remember seeing is roller skating. Is that a deal breaker?"

"I only roller skated on Fridays at the drum circle."

"Knowing Bend the way I do, I will wager there is a roller blading scene out there somewhere. You'll fit right in."

"Should I go home and get my clothes and stuff?"

"Let's get you to Bend asap. You can go clothes shopping out there. There's Lulu's Boutique, Jubeelee, Hot Box Betty—start with those. Get some yoga gear. Anyone who doesn't go to yoga classes in Bend is viewed with suspicion. You'll want to blend in Bend. Hold it. I like the sound of that, too. 'Have you been to Bend? Did you blend in Bend?' I love this whole idea more and more. I want to get out there in May for the Pole Pedal Paddle. Or maybe the Flagline 50K. Whooooeeee! Am I excited! Let's get you to Charlotte and on a plane to Bend. Stay at a hotel on the company dime until you find a place to rent. Get yourself situated. I will be out there quicker than you can say Pole Pedal Paddle. And our first stop? Deschutes Brewery. You have not lived until you've had their juniper elk burger with a Black Butte Porter.

I'm going crazy just thinking about it. Can't wait to get out there."

"What's my job? What do I do once I get settled?"

McGrogan opened a black satchel and pulled out a photograph of a young, former A-list Hollywood actor whose career hit a few speed bumps lately.

"Know this guy?" McGrogan asked.

"Yes, isn't that…?"

"Shhhhh. We are an organization that prides itself on discretion, darling. We communicate through nods and gestures. Loose lips sink ships."

"So he's famous? That's the one?"

"He's living out in Bend. A few Hollywood types had local construction guys build them craftsmen bungalow. The skiing's good. Plenty of pretty girls. They think they're hiding in plain sight. Enough beautiful fit people live in Bend that a hundred guys look like they could make living in Hollywood. He is a client of ours, an asset, if you will, and he's sort of gone off the reservation. He might have enough juice to get away with this rather adolescent behavior with the studio chiefs, but Daddy here does not play those games."

"What do I have to do with him?"

"Try to get close to him. See where his head's at. I'll text you details about his daily routine as soon as you get out there."

"You really think he's going to notice me?"

"Honey, you'll head right to the top of the class in any city anywhere. He will notice you."

"What do I do after he notices me?"

"Be my eyes and ears in Bend. He's been disloyal. Thinks he can jerk me around like he's probably jerked everybody else around since kindergarten. He's a pampered brat. I'd like to have him back in the fold because I've already pulled a lot of strings for him. Opened a lot of doors. But when it came to gratitude time, I discovered he was all out of gratitude. Didn't plan to keep his end of the bargain. I will send you further instructions once you get situated. No rush. He's not going anywhere. If he is, you will go with him. Enjoy all the outdoor beauty Bend has to offer."

At the pep rally on Friday afternoon, the fall athletic teams were feted. A DJ played music. The principal gave a speech about how athletics doesn't build character, it reveals it. The marching band played from the bleachers. The freshmen teams were acknowledged to polite applause. Captains of the varsity soccer, cross country, field hockey, and football teams spoke. The dance team and cheer squads performed their latest routines. A contest was held to see which grade cheered the loudest. Finally, a game of musical chairs was played between representatives of each of the varsity teams. Oxley didn't take part in any of the spotlight activities. He came out when the "rest of the varsity football team" was called in from the hallway to center court. It was the last activity involving the football team this season that didn't involve the spotlight being on Oxley.

The team headed to Clayton that evening to face the Clippers in the season opener. Clayton was a small public high school that had a top-notch wrestling program and a number of excellent football teams through the years. In the 1980s, Clayton won the state championship in basketball. The first quarter ended with Clayton leading 6-0. Disaster nearly struck the Lions in the second quarter, when starting defensive back Jeff Jackson suffered a serious knee injury and was taken to a local hospital. Jackson was the Lions' best defender against the pass and was their second string halfback on offense.

Oxley had yet to see any action, but when the Lions held the Clippers on fourth and goal from the 3-yard line, he was inserted at halfback. The coaches would not risk passing in this precarious field position and liked the fact that Oxley had never fumbled. They planned to run the ball up the middle three times and hoped that their offensive line would clear holes big enough for Oxley to pick up a first down so they could briefly rest their first string halfback, Ray Mergens. Mergens played linebacker on defense and had just been instrumental in stopping Clayton near the goal line. Clayton and Gloucester played a number of their better athletes on both sides of the ball, and toward the end of the half, they were fatigued. Oxley took a handoff on the Gloucester 3-yard line and immediately went 97 yards for a Lions touchdown. No one had laid a hand on him and he got down the field so fast that some people wondered if they were dreaming. The Clayton coaches were baffled. Even a couple of the Gloucester coaches were baffled. Oxley was sent back in for the two-point conversion and scored easily, running around the end untouched. The Lions went into halftime leading 8-6.

When the Lions came out of the locker room for the second half, fans were yelling "Put Oxley in" to the coaches on the sideline. Oxley played a third of the Lions offensive plays in the second half and scored two more touchdowns. The final score was Gloucester 32-Clayton 20. The game wasn't as close as the score indicated. The Lions substitutes played the entire fourth quarter. After the victory, The Gloucester Lions gathered by the end zone, raised their helmets, and sang, as Lions football teams had for decades:

"That good ol' Gloucester spirit,
That good ol' Gloucester spirit,
That good ol' Gloucester spirit,
It's good enough for me."

Then the Lions knelt on one knee in their end zone and Coach Claiborn said:

"Big step in the right direction tonight. I'm proud of you guys. When Jeff got hurt, everybody stepped up their game. That's what winners do. I like the feel of this team. You stick together. You stand behind each other. Don't go patting each other on the back yet. We won one game. It's a long season. We played tough, hard-nosed Gloucester football against another tough group of kids. Everyone is going to be telling you how great you are when you get home tonight. Maintain your edge. Stay hungry. We took one step, that's all. We have a ton of work to do and we have to stay business-like and focused. We'll watch films of the game tomorrow, off on Sunday, and then four days to get ready for Glassboro. Glassboro will be a stiffer test. Stay humble and hungry. Deflect the compliments. We will all know in late November if we were any good this season or not."

The Lions game only drew a one-line mention in the newspapers the next day: "John Oxley gained 213 yards on 9 carries to lead Gloucester over Clayton, 32-20." The headlines went to the Top Ten teams, bigger schools like Cherokee, Camden Catholic, Delsea, Kingsway, St. Augustine, and Group 1 superpower, Paulsboro. Gloucester's program had fallen out of the elite, and the win against Clayton was viewed as inconsequential by local sportswriters.

Oxley walked to the high school to watch film of the game on Saturday. He arrived early as he always did. No one was in the locker room and he walked down C-wing to the classroom where the team viewed films. He passed the trainer's room on the way and Coach Claiborn was sitting on the trainer's table with a big bag of ice on each knee, still nursing injuries he received on the college gridiron over forty years ago. Oxley walked in to say hello.

"Good game, dude."

"Thanks, Coach."

"I guess I better put you in more or they'll be hanging me in effigy."

"No need for that. I'm just happy to contribute."

"You know, John, you're probably the first guy ever to say that to me and actually mean it," he laughed. "You did get a whole lot better, buddy. We'll start getting you that ball more. You enjoying it?"

"It's a lot different, that's for sure."

"Alright. See you down the hall. Let me take care of these old knees. If I was a horse, they'd shoot me."

The team watched the film of the Clayton game and the coaches pointed out many ways they could improve with better execution, better discipline, and more precision with their pass routes. The Lions started six sophomores who made sophomore mistakes. The players had agreed to stay sober and adhere to curfews for the length of the football season. Some players interpreted "stay sober" as an agreement not to drink any alcoholic beverages during the season, and some interpreted it more loosely. "Don't let your personal issues become team issues," Coach Claiborn said. The curfews were a commitment to be at their own house by 10:00 on weeknights and 11:00 on weekends. The coaches did not check up on the curfew; they appealed to the players' honor. Weekend parties were a long-standing tradition in Gloucester, and the curfew and sobriety pledges were a test of the players' maturity and dedication. Part of the reason the program had stumbled these past few years was that some players were getting trashed every Friday and Saturday night. An assistant coach reminded the team of their commitment and asked them to keep the focus of their lives on football and their studies for the next ten weeks.

"You have the rest of your life for everything else," he said.

Consequently, there weren't any parties that night. Oxley had never partied with the football team anyway, but kids made plans to watch college football games at their friend's house, to play video games, or to go to the movies with their girlfriends. A few teammates invited Oxley to these activities, but he had decided to devote his Saturday night to practicing the sax. Mike King dropped him off at his house, and from there Oxley walked to Joe's Pizzeria for dinner. He sat at the counter and asked for change for a dollar so he could feed the jukebox.

"Oxley-boy," Nick said. "I just read about you in the paper. Never knew you were any good at football."

"I'm not."

"Must be pretty good if they're writing about you in the newspaper."

"Yeah, it's weird."

"Don't go getting a big head."

Angie showed up to work the dinner shift. Seeing Oxley, she said, "Heard you're a football star, Oxley."

"Of sorts," he laughed.

"Another game like that and I'll be asking for your autograph."

Oxley enjoyed the food and music and walked back home to practice. As he walked, he felt his phone vibrate in his pocket. It was a text from Barb. He felt relieved and excited. The he read the message:

"Why is Devan sitting on your front steps?"

"I'm walking back from Joe's. I had no idea she was at my house. And if you hadn't blocked me, we could have talked this out already. You ignore me in school. I can't text you. Why don't I walk to your house and we can talk? I care about you. I don't want this tension between us."

"You created the tension. And I can't see you this evening because we have play practice. I'm getting ready to leave. Have fun with your little ratchet."

"Just don't block me on your phone. We can talk later."

"Bite me."

Oxley walked to his house and intended to tell Devan that he had to rehearse. His Rutgers audition was approaching. When he arrived, he saw that she was crying.

"What's the matter?"

"I can't find my dog. He got out of the yard and I've been running around in circles. I don't know the street grid of the town yet. I keep passing the same landmarks over and over again. Will you help me?"

"I can drive around for about an hour, but then I have something important to do that I can't get out of. What street do you live on?"

"We're renting a place on King Street, down by the river. There's a park across the street where I usually walk him. I'm hoping he marked it enough times that he'll return there. I've checked around my neighborhood but I keep getting disoriented. I love that little guy. He's been with me through thick and thin."

"What does he look like? What breed is he?"

"He's a grey Cairn Terrier. His name's 'Ozzie.'"

Oxley got into Devan's Jetta and they drove down Hudson Street to King Street. They searched the Freedom Pier area. It was a wide expanse of land that housed the headquarters of Holt Logistics, a large shipping firm that imports fruit from South America and distributes it throughout the Philadelphia metropolitan region. Holt leased the land from the city, and it remained an open space for the public. Holt occupied a building that was previously the headquarters of the U.S. Coast Guard. Holt owned most of the land in the city that bordered the Delaware River. Oxley's mom was one of hundreds of people from Gloucester who worked at Holt. Freedom Pier was a bricked walkway where people exercised, read, and watched the river flow. You can see the neighboring towns of Brooklawn, Westville, and National Park from the pier. Oxley and Devan walked around the perimeter and headed along the river south to Proprietor's Park. There was a long fishing pier that was busy even on a September Saturday evening. There was no sign of Ozzie. Devan called his name as they walked through the park to a fishing marina at the park's southern edge. They got back in her car and traveled down Jersey Avenue toward Dolson's Tavern on the Edge, a popular restaurant.

"How about you drive so I can yell out the window?"

She pulled the car into the curb in front of Dolson's and they got out and switched seats. He enjoyed driving the Jetta, even slowly, as Devan screamed "Ozzie, Ozzie" up and down the streets that jutted off Jersey Avenue. It started to get dark. They swung down Broadway, turned into the CVS parking lot, and swung back down Jersey toward King Street. They made a right onto King Street and parked in front of Devan's house. Her house had a wrought-iron gate beside the front steps and they heard the manic barking of the little grey terrier echoing through the car windows. Devan hurled herself out of the car, opened the gate, and hugged the dog to her chest.

"My baby, my baby," she exclaimed as Ozzie licked her face over and over. Oxley got out and stood beside her until the reunion ran out of steam.

"You better put some chicken wire or something on the bottom two feet of your gate. He can squeeze right through. He got out by himself and he got back in by himself. There's too much traffic along King Street to let that happen again. You love him. It's going to be a disaster if you don't find a way to block that gate."

The side of the house was separated from a neighboring business by a solid wood privacy fence. The wrought-iron gate was handsome but wasn't designed to contain a small dog. Devan put the dog in the house while Oxley sat out in the car and texted Barb.

"I miss you. I feel unmoored without you. All of the stuff with D. was totally random. She sat across from me in the cafeteria before I even knew she was there. I didn't even know her name at the time. She was at the school for some reason when we came out of practice one day and I unconsciously took a ride home with her. Nothing happened. She was on my steps this evening because her dog was lost and she couldn't navigate the streets to find him because she's only lived here a short while. As soon as we found the dog, I went home. Text me later if you can. Please. I am willing to completely cut myself off from her if that's what it will take to get back to what we used to have. She is nothing to me. You are everything."

"Dude, did you just express positive emotion for me? It's a Christmas miracle and it's not even Christmas! I'm walking home now. Play practice sucked. Talk with you soon."

Devan came out and hopped into the passenger side again.

"You might as well keep driving," she said. "We can switch when we get back to your house. Thanks so much for chasing after my crazy dog. You're really a good friend, you know that?"

Oxley enjoyed the feeling of being behind the wheel of such a sweet car. His mom drove a five-year-old Dodge Caravan. It wasn't worth borrowing. He drove down Monmouth Street and was sitting at the red light at Broadway when his throat sank through his chest. Barb had walked with her friends to Cabana Water Ice on Broadway and was walking toward the intersection. Oxley's armpits felt like lava. He felt moisture on his neck. Seconds ticked by like minutes. He hoped that by some good fortune he could get across Broadway before Barb spotted him behind the wheel of Devan's Jetta. He didn't. Their eyes met just as the light changed to green, and a soft serve chocolate ice cream cone whizzed by the driver's side window. He checked the side view mirror to see Barb with both middle fingers extended as he pulled away. After getting dropped off, Oxley checked his phone right away.

"Lose my number," was all it said.

Life accelerates for high school students the second week of September. Assignments are due. Quizzes and tests become part of the normal class routine. Papers are assigned. The summer stupor is shed and anyone serious about getting good grades shifts into gear. Oxley enjoyed learning and he enjoyed the competition of the AP classes. In the AP courses, he felt that he was competing with students across the country, not just those in Gloucester. He was intent on accumulating as many college credits as possible to trim tuition costs and to allow more time in his college schedule to take music courses. He was still trying to adjust to Barb not speaking to him. It was a major adjustment. They had been firm allies for years both in and out of the classroom. Even worse, the majority of girls in his class sided with Barb and were frostier and less friendly than ever to him. His stock had gone up with the boys at school, but Oxley preferred the company of Barb.

Devan sat across from him every day in the cafeteria. He had no way to prevent it. The other boys at his table tried to catch her attention and she would smile briefly to anyone who spoke with her, then return her focus to Oxley. Students returned from summer break with tans but Devan's was world class. She had spent the summer on Florida beaches and had a dark bronze hue. He hair was dark and thick and cascaded past her shoulders. Her eyes were golden brown. She carried a Kate Spade laptop bag and a Gucci Nymphea handbag. Her fingernails were painted to perfection. Her smile was flawless. Any single one of these traits would be a reason for a number of girls at Gloucester High to dislike her; taken together, they cemented her role as the least popular female in the high school. She didn't care. She didn't even seem to notice.

Barb alternated between constructing revenge fantasies involving Devan, revenge fantasies involving Oxley, and assuring herself that she would find much more compatible guys when she went away to college. She thought about looking for a job but didn't want to relinquish control over how she dressed, her makeup, and her hair. Her mom suggested she put her art skills to work at a tattoo parlor.

"That would be like an alcoholic working as a bartender. Can you imagine how many tattoos I'd have before I graduated from high school? I'd probably run out of skin. The only thing that stops me now is lack of cash and lack of access. I'd have both and you'd be begging me to quit after two weeks."

Barb practiced her piano with her usual fervor. She expanded her repertoire, adding some Red Garland tunes and "Misterioso" by Thelonious Monk. She ignored Oxley— except for all the time she thought about him.

Football practices revved into a higher gear. After a month of practice, players were efficient and direct in their movements on both sides of the ball. Practices were livelier and the coaches weren't blowing the whistle every thirty seconds to point out a blown assignment, improper alignment, or careless error. The team was adrenalized from the win over Clayton. Glassboro was a bigger challenge than Clayton. Glassboro football had a long, storied history. The football team had won the South Jersey state sectional championships in 1974, 1975, 1981, 1983, 1987, 1999, 2007, 2008, 2010, 2011, and 2013. Gary Brackett, the great linebacker of the Super Bowl XLI champion Indianapolis Colts, was a former Glassboro High player. Gordon Lockbaum, a running back who twice finished in the top five in the Heisman Trophy balloting, was a former Glassboro Bulldog. Current Tampa Bay Buccaneer defensive end George Johnson played his high school football for Glassboro. Glassboro provided a steady flow of running backs to D1, D2, and D3 college football programs. The Bulldogs opened their season with a decisive victory over Wildwood. Coach Claiborn addressed the team after final practice preparations Thursday:

"Glassboro will be out to prove a point tomorrow night. The newspapers predict that they're down this year. It will be a statement game for one team or the other. It's going to separate the contender from the pretender. Be proud of wearing the Gloucester uniform. Plenty of great people who came before you were very proud to wear it. Get good rest tonight, and let's be ready to rock them tomorrow."

The game was at Glassboro. Coach Claiborn insisted on silence on the ride to away games. The focus was on their opponent. Both teams were hoping to prove they were better this season than the sportswriters had predicted. The Lions won the toss and elected to receive. The Bulldogs stopped them after they picked up two first downs and had moved the ball to midfield. The Bulldogs managed a sustained march that was stopped at the Lions 20. The Bulldogs attempted a field goal on fourth down and missed; the Lions took over. Oxley entered the game and three plays later entered the end zone. The Lions offense was crisp. They scored on four consecutive possessions. Oxley finished the game with 279 yards rushing on thirteen carries. The Lions won 40-16. Oxley was the leading scorer in all of South Jersey despite having carried the ball twenty-two times in two games. The next day's newspapers noted his rushing stats but devoted only a sentence to the outcome of the game. The Lions were 2-0 for the first time in six seasons and would face the Pitman Panthers the following Friday evening in their first home game of the 2016 season.

The first in an eventual torrent of recruiting letters for Oxley began to arrive. He heard from Division 3 schools Rowan, The College of New Jersey, Wesley, Widener, Gettysburg, and William Patterson. The letters went to Coach Claiborn, and on Wednesday Oxley was called down to the athletic director's office to discuss his options at this point.

"You're playing pretty well, dude. People are starting to notice. You interested in playing college football? I remember you telling me last year you wanted be a musician, right? Will that jibe with playing a sport in college? Are you interested?

You have a pretty unique talent. And it seems like you're getting better each week."

"Do these schools offer scholarships?"

"These schools do not offer scholarships. They do offer need-based financial aid. What're your family finances like, you have any idea?"

"I assume the finances are good," Oxley said. "My mom's a food safety inspector at Holt's. I never met my dad. My mom has moved up the ranks at her company. She's smart and always pushes me to go to college. I assume she has money saved. We live in the house she grew up in, so there's no mortgage. I think my grandparents let us live there. That's all I know about our finances."

"So your mom probably has money put aside for your education. That would be great. You can make a decision about college without worrying that you'd have to do anything to earn a scholarship."

"Thanks. My top priority is to go somewhere with a good music program. I don't know if I want to play football or not."

"Well, this is probably just the beginning of the recruiting letters. These are the local guys. When people hear about your foot speed and power, it's going to attract a bunch of schools, maybe even some big ones."

"I'll think about it."

"You happy with the way things are going?"

"I like that we're winning. I hope we can keep it going. I'm fine with how many carries I'm getting. I appreciate it a lot that you treated me the same way the past three seasons when I was pretty terrible as you do this season. I always felt respected by you. That counts for more than anything to me. I'm completely good with whatever you want to do."

"I can see how talented you are, John. The more people coaches can keep happy, the better for team spirit. We've got a lot of guys happy right now. When we start playing the bigger schools like Delsea and Kingsway, you'll probably be called on more. And you'll be fresh. That's something else to think about. You aren't getting beat up week after week."

"I like things exactly the way they are. It's great to contribute."

The Pitman game was a laugher. Gloucester's JVs played most of the second half. Oxley carried the ball nine times for 201 yards. There was a big crowd out for the first home game and people hoped a return to Gloucester's glory days was possible. After Pitman, the Lions had a bye week and Coach Claiborn gave them off from practice Monday, Tuesday, and Saturday. They would watch films on Sunday evening. Oxley decided to devote the three days off to practicing for his audition and rebuilding his connection with Barb.

He knew she had play practice on Saturday and would be gone until after dinner. He went to the flower shop and bought a small bouquet of roses, lilies, and daisies. He was walking to her house in Gloucester Heights and ran into a few Gloucester High basketball players at the public basketball courts. Two of them walked to the side of the court where a tall, chain link fence separated the court from the sidewalk.

"You got flowers for that girl Devan? Must be hoping for some fireworks later on."

"I'm actually trying to make up with someone else."

"Not that crazy looking chick from the band?"

"Yes."

"The one with purple hair and shit?"

"Different strokes for different folks, brother."

Oxley walked away and continued to Barb's. He walked to her house and waited on the front steps. He liked how insulated from the rest of the world he felt around Barb. They were kindred spirits. He waited a long half hour and saw her turn off Nicholson Road toward her house. She was with a group of kids from the marching band. Something looked amiss though. The part of his brain that makes sense of symbols and shapes searched for what looked unfamiliar. Then it struck him. Barb was holding hands and laughing with another musician, a drummer from the marching band named Kirk Wessner. Oxley felt a sense of brief panic but decided to walk away in the other direction before the group arrived. He left the flowers on the porch and started walking double-time.

"Hey, Oxley," yelled Barb, holding the flowers aloft. "Did you forget something?"

Oxley walked down Nicholson Road and pondered his options. He felt like a spear had pierced his chest. How did he not realize he liked Barb so much? Was he *that* damaged? What was wrong with him anyway? Why did it take this kind of shit storm to realize how nice he had it before? He could not remember a time when he felt worse. It was agonizing. When he walked past the basketball courts, kids yelled to him:

"That was quick, Oxley. What'd you change your mind? Smart move, dude."

Oxley didn't turn his head to acknowledge that he heard them. He went home and grabbed his sax but put it down without playing a note. He sat on the couch and tried to calm his thoughts. He couldn't. When he could no longer stand the pain, he impulsively sought a human distraction, in the person of Devan DeBree. He felt like he was suffocating. He texted Devan:

"What are you up to?"

"Sitting around listening to music. I'm bored. My mom went to Philly for the night. Want me to pick you up?"

"That would be great. Thanks."

About ten minutes later, Devan pulled up in the Jetta and away they went.

"I'm not in the best of moods," he said. "I apologize in advance."

"No worries. I have plenty of cures for that."

"I'm so jammed up."

"You're so uptight. There are many ways to relax in this world, but you don't ever seem interested in relaxing. It's like you're walking down the same narrow alley every day with the same people. No wonder you feel jammed up."

They pulled up to Devan's house and walked in. Devan said her mom rented the place on a month-to-month lease. The house was a twin in the historic, older part of Gloucester City. It faced Proprietor's Park and a narrow slip of the Delaware River. Hardwood floors and large windows designed to maximize the view of the river were its best assets. Artwork hung on every wall—original Mexican paintings by Fernando Olivera, a few Klee prints, and a signed Peter Max. Devan flopped on a Kelston sectional sofa. Oxley sat across the room in an Eames lounge chair. He began to unconsciously rock in short, nervous bursts.

"You isolate, that's your problem. You're even isolated now here with me. Look at you! If you wanted a distraction, why didn't you just watch a movie? Come over here a minute. Let me massage your shoulders."

Oxley got up and half-heartedly sat next to Devan on the sofa. She grabbed his upper arms and spun him away from her so she could knead his shoulders. She spoke to him as she worked her thumb into his upper back.

"You're way too tense. Did your little band paramour get tired of waiting for you to thaw out? Did she find another object for her affections?"

"I don't want to talk about it."

"Of course not! Then you'd be a human being with human feelings. How terrible that must be, right? Let her take her bad moods somewhere else. You've got enough of your own."

"I wasn't even aware that I cared about her that much."

Devan punched his back sharply with the side of her fist.

"You've got knots on top of knots, Oxley. You should go to a masseuse. You'll need to find one of those strong Eastern European woman like the ones in Miami Beach. Those ladies dig right down to your rib cage."

"I don't know what I need."

"I know what you need—let's have one of my mom's special brownies and listen to some music. Sound good? Do you want a soda or anything?"

Devan brought in a plate of brownies and two drinks. She turned off the table lamp and fiddled with her phone. Her stereo came to life and the album *A Good Night in the Ghetto* by Kamaiyah streamed through the speakers.

"Nice set up, " said Oxley, nodding toward the stereo speakers.

"You band guys aren't the only people who appreciate music. Let me introduce you to twenty-first-century music. There's so much great stuff."

They ate the brownies and Oxley began to relax.

"The music's amazing."

"Let me program some stuff so it just keeps streaming."

She grabbed her phone. "Let's hear Chance the Rapper, Gucci Mane, A$AP Mob, Ant Beale, Isaiah Rashad, and A Tribe Called Quest. You need some schooling, young'un."

The music washed over him, and Oxley felt he was melting into the sofa. He watched the lights of ships and tugboats flicker through the window as they sailed down the Delaware. He forgot where he was and before long, he was locked in a steamy embrace with Devan. He woke up hours later lying on the sofa next to Devan. He leaned over Devan's sleeping body and retrieved his phone. It was 1 a.m. He gently hopped over Devan and put his jeans and sandals back on, tiptoed to her front door, and let himself out. He walked down King Street to Monmouth and as he turned, a police car pulled up along-side him.

The cop rolled down the passenger side window.

"Do you know how late it is, son? It's three hours past the city curfew."

"I'm sorry. I fell asleep at my friend's house. I'm walking home now."

"John?" It was one of the police officers he saw once or twice at the PAL Club.

"Yes, I'm really sorry."

"Hop in, I'll drive you home before someone sees you and tells Coach Claiborn."

"Oh, snap. I never even thought about that."

"Look at your neck!! Looks like you were doing more than sleeping. Man, I wish I could relive those days. You're living the life, buddy. Savor it. Ten years from now, you'll be like me, punching the clock every day with a couple of kids and a pile of bills. Enjoy it while it lasts."

Oxley blushed about the mark on his neck, worried about the football coaches finding out about his late hours, and wondered just what had happened back at Devan's. He could hear the police officer's voice but wasn't absorbing the words. He thanked the officer, went into his house and found a mirror. He felt relieved. One strawberry-shaped mark, deep purple, right above his collarbone. If he wore a hoodie, the mark would be out of sight. He sat down and stared out the window. He wasn't sleepy. His head felt cloudy and confused.

Barb's mom drove to see her father every Sunday. Barb sat with her while she was getting dressed in her bedroom.

"Will you ask Daddy if I can come next week?"

"I will ask him, but he doesn't want you to see him incarcerated. He's ashamed."

"I miss him."

"He misses you."

"So you'll ask him if I can visit?"

"Yes."

"Why did he have so much on him? It was enough meth for an entire city."

"We've been over this before. Barb. Your father was trying to pick up extra money by selling stimulants to other truckers. The demand for stimulants is strong because those guys drive twelve to sixteen hours at a stretch. It's inhuman, especially when you start to get up in years a little. The pills are invigorating. It's not like they are partying. They're driving from New Jersey to Florida."

"Red Bull doesn't do the trick?"

"Not for driving fourteen straight hours, plus it makes you stop to go to the bathroom. The drivers prefer pills. Daddy was one of many guys who provided them. It was a clean, easy way of bringing home more money to you and me. Truck drivers don't get paid what they're worth. All those hours on the highways in all kinds of crazy weather. Daddy regrets it deeply, and if he could redo those years, he would. He misses you terribly. He's missed out on so much."

"Why did he have a handgun on him if he was just picking up some extra clean, easy money?"

"Who said he had a handgun on him?"

"The Department of Corrections website."

"You shouldn't be snooping on the DOC website, Barb. He needed a gun for protection. So he didn't get robbed."

"Sounds like it wasn't all that clean and easy, Mom, if his clientele was unstable enough that he needed a handgun for protection. Sounds kind of crazy."

"The *Bible* says don't judge."

"I'm not judging. Jeez. I just wish it hadn't of happened. I don't hold it against him. I miss him. I want to go see him. I feel like I don't know him and that he no longer knows me."

"I'll talk to your dad. I tell him about your many triumphs, Barb. Your dad is as proud as can be, especially how you've managed to keep striving without him, and with me working a lot."

"It hasn't been easy."

"I'm sure it hasn't. Where's Oxley been, anyway? You two were inseparable. Now he's never around. Did you have a falling out?"

"I don't want to talk about it."

'Uh oh."

"Yeah, uh oh. Please don't bring it up again."

Devan texted Oxley first thing Sunday morning.

"You ok? I woke up and you were gone."

"I'm confused, as always."

"You weren't confused last night. Seemed like you forgot yourself for once."

"I'm even confused about why I'm confused."

"You think too much. Let's do something later."

"I have some stuff I have to get done for school first. I will text you later, I promise."

"You better."

Oxley had homework that he had neglected, forcing him to play catch up with school work. He did most school projects on the day they were assigned for the past eleven years. When he completed his academic obligations, he felt compelled to pick up his sax. He hadn't played in days. But he felt no particular motivation to play now. He texted Devan, hoping he'd feel inspired to practice after lunch.

"You want to get lunch some place?"

"Sure. Want me to pick you up?"

Joe's was closed on Sundays, so they drove to 10th and Christian Street in South Philadelphia to Santucci's, makers of the best pizza in Philadelphia. On the way over the Walt Whitman Bridge, they talked about popular music. Devan felt Lil Wayne and Eminem were geniuses, every bit as great as John Lennon or John Coltrane. They talked about movies. Oxley felt that as an art form, cinema had peaked in the '60s and '70s.

"You think *everything* peaked in the '60s and '70s," Devan protested. They parked behind St. Paul's Church and walked to Santucci's, ordered a pizza, and talked.

"How could you have been with Barb all those times, all those years, and not realize you were in love with her?"

"I didn't know what love was. I don't think I'd be who I am without my friendship with her. She introduced me to so many joys and pleasures, things that inform me, that make me who I am. It's weird that another person can do that but she did. I don't regret any of it. I regret not realizing it wouldn't continue forever."

"I don't get it. You never had the urge to kiss her?"

"I fantasized about it a lot."

"But you never got around to doing it."

"I'm awkward. And she's awkward. I think both of us were afraid to go there for fear it would complicate to contaminate our friendship and I couldn't imagine surviving high school without our friendship. It was just about all I had for a long while. That and my music."

"I'm just the opposite. I dive into a physical relationship first and then figure out along the way if I like them. My body directs me. You are sealed off in your mind."

"That's what you're doing with me?"

"Probably," she laughed. "But I already knew I liked you. You're different. You're an old soul, Oxley. You know what I like best about you? You don't try to use me for anything."

"Other people have used you?"

"Used and abused."

"But you're completely beautiful. Why would you allow that?"

"It's a long story. And we're talking about you."

"Not exactly my favorite topic."

"What's your game plan for getting Barb back?"

"If you like me, how can you be encouraging me to try to win Barb back?"

"Oxley, I'm moving away from here soon. I've got a month-to-month lease. Do you really think I'm naive enough to suppose you'll drop everything and follow me to Pascagoula, Mississippi, or wherever I'm off to next? I'll be lucky you remember me a week after I'm gone."

"I'll remember you. How can I forget you after last night?"

"Hopefully last night was an awakening. But I sort of doubt it. I had to practice a bit of voodoo to get you there."

After they ate their pizza, they walked to a used books and record store in the Italian Market on 9th Street. It was Oxley's favorite store on Earth, but the store stirred up memories of Barb so the visit was brief. They drove back to Gloucester, and Devan dropped Oxley off at the high school.

The team was watching films of their next opponent, the Kingsway Dragons. The tough part of the season was about to begin. Gloucester would play three much larger schools, Kingsway, Williamstown, and Delsea, in the next three weeks. Oxley hoped to have another opportunity to speak with Coach Claiborn. He walked past the old gym and saw that the light was on in the trainer's room. Once again, Coach Claiborn was sitting on the trainer's bench, icing his knees after walking a few miles on the track.

"Hey John."

"Hey Coach Claiborn. How're the knees?"

"Old war wounds, buddy. Hopefully, you never have any. So far, so good, dude. I don't think you can get hurt unless someone tackles you. They've had a hard time doing that with you. You're a lot quicker than I was."

"Yeah, but you were great."

The coach laughed. "You're not doing too bad yourself, Johnny."

"Thanks."

"It's gonna be different from here on out though. Just like we're studying films about Kingsway today, they're going to be studying films about us. And when they do, the coaches are going to tell their guys that the game's gonna come down to whether or not they can stop John Oxley. We've been using you judiciously but most coaches are smart enough to realize that you've become our main weapon."

"I appreciate the little break. And it will feel good to get back to regular practice this week."

"The advantage big schools like Kingsway, Delsea, Williamstown, and Clearview have is depth. Their players aren't necessarily any better than ours. In fact, our top guys this year are better than their top guys. But we only play seventeen or eighteen kids usually. They play thirty kids and they're all pretty decent. We have six hundred kids in our high school. They have eleven hundred. It makes a big difference. The state athletic association is developing a plan so that Group 1 schools would only play Group 1 schools, Group 2 play Group 2, and so forth. What the hell's that on your neck?"

"Ahhhhhhhhh…."

"Thought you were the quiet bookworm musician type!"

Oxley blushed down to his heels.

"All right, dude. See you in the classroom."

Oxley adjusted the folds of his hoodie to cover his neck better before walking into the classroom of teammates.

By Wednesday, they were practicing again. Barb spoke animatedly to her friends about how extraordinary and interesting her boyfriend was, and Oxley had no choice but to endure it. He did stop camouflaging the mark on his neck as a gesture of retaliation. And he continued to enjoy Devan's company. Oxley was fascinated by Devan's detachment. She didn't want to talk about anything except the present moment. She offered good insights. She didn't care who liked her and who didn't like her. He was frustrated because he was stifling his feelings for Barb but because he was so busy, it was less tortuous. Devan assured him that patience was the smart strategy.

"You can't change another person, Oxley. That's not possible. But at some point, Barb's going to realize that the little drummer boy is not her type exactly and she'll be open again to the possibility of you and her living happily ever after. Don't try to force it. It will happen organically if you don't contaminate it by acting like an idiot. Just let it be."

The Kingsway game arrived with the first week of October. The game was in Gloucester. The *Philadelphia Inquirer*, the *Courier-Post*, and the *South Jersey Times* each sent a reporter to cover it. Reporter Scott Chapolone covered the game for the *South Jersey Times*:

> *John Oxley has been kept under wraps so far this football season, but Friday evening he had his coming out party. Oxley, a senior who has yet to start a game for the young Lions, amassed impressive rushing numbers on limited carries in the Lions three victories over Clayton, Glassboro, and Pitman. Coach Lee Claiborn unleashed Oxley last evening and the slender running back gained a massive 403 yards on 29 carries against a very good Kingsway team. Oxley was simply unstoppable in the Lions 40-20 victory. "He's something special," Claiborn said. "Maybe once in a lifetime special. I've never seen a guy ever improve so much from one season to the next. He's much faster, much stronger, much more elusive. We have plenty of tough tests coming up but Kingsway is pretty darn good. He's a hard guy to tackle. The best thing about him is that he's humble and coachable. He's also a terrific student. He's a great kid. Glad he's wearing the Blue and Gold."*

For the first time, reporters were waiting to speak with Oxley after the game. They asked him what was his favorite class. What was his favorite food in the high school cafeteria? What did he like best about Gloucester High? He was respectful and polite. Afterwards, he turned his phone off and spent the night at Devan's. It was easier than worrying about getting caught out after curfew.

Devan, known as Renee Bauman during her time in Bend, fell in love with the Hollywood actor. They jogged together. They went on long bike rides. They hung out listening to jazz at 10Below at the Oxford. They took a cooking class together at The Well Traveled Fork. In September, on the one-hundred-day anniversary of meeting McGrogan, a well-dressed man surprised Devan as she left her hot yoga class at Jupiter Yoga on Revere Avenue and asked her to sign a contract promising her employment to Fly By Night Enterprises and McGrogan "until death do us part." Devan signed without hesitation. Three months ago, she was a wall flower at Asheville High School. Now she was on the arm of a handsome movie star and living a life she could not have dreamed. She attributed McGrogan's "until death do us part" line to his flair for the dramatic. Winter came early, and by Thanksgiving they were skiing every weekend along the trails at Virginia Meissner. On Christmas Eve, they were enjoying a gluten-free, vegetarian dinner at 900 Wall, the choice of Hollywood expats residing in Bend. The restaurant was housed in a magnificent, charming 1920s building that felt perfect for the holiday. Devan and her actor friend were seated at a secluded table for four in a hidden corner of the main dining room when McGrogan appeared.

"Then one foggy Christmas Eve, Santa came to say...."

"McGrogan. What the hell? What are you doing here?" the actor asked, choking on his kale.

"Then one foggy Christmas Eve, Santa came to say.... What Santa's come to say is, wherefore art thou, Jonny? Don't you have promises to keep?"

"Dude, I've dropped out of that whole Hollywood scene. It's all bullshit. I'm living a regular life. I've found a beautiful woman...."

"Or she's found you," McGrogan said.

"Whatever, dude. I dropped out. I've got a new life now."

"Jon, if I remember correctly, you came up in farm country. What do you think a farmer would do if he went out one morning and all of his cows told him they 'dropped out?' Think he might be pissed?"

"I don't care if you're pissed. I ain't going back. After a while, I felt like I was on a plantation."

"Now, Jon, that's a bit of a stretch for a White millionaire who was living in a gated community in Calabasas. You're giving me a neck cramp."

"I want to forget that whole part of my life."

"Seems to me that you've forgotten the part where you were about to be charged with felony possession of a firearm, criminal mischief, and aggravated assault by the Los Angeles District Attorney. If it wasn't for me, Jon, you'd probably be enjoying a vacation in a jail cell instead of the Pacific Northwest health and wellness capital."

"Excuse me, I've got to hit the bathroom."

Jon walked away in a huff.

"Darling, I think it's time for our boot heels to be wandering."

"What do you mean? I don't want to leave. I love him. I've watched him day and night for you."

"Honey, I've decided to downsize my Bend, Oregon, operation. I can offer you a position in one of my many other company locales. Perhaps you're ready for a sunnier clime? It does get chilly up here. Makes my neck cramp."

"What about Jon?"

"Jon has gone to join his forefathers, darling. My advice to you, as your mentor, is to catch the first flight out of Bend before those pesky cops start showing up wondering what happen to Jonny. They always seem to start questioning the person who saw him last. Spotlight's on you, kiddo. Let's scram."

"I want to see him. I'll talk to him when he comes back from the bathroom. Maybe he'll listen to me."

"Honeybunch, Jonny's not coming back from the bathroom. Breach of contract is a serious offense. It hurts me because I had him positioned to be a person of great influence, but you gotta know when to hold 'em, and know when to fold 'em. And I just folded my hand of young Jon. I was tiring of his disrespect, to be perfectly honest. I'm sensitive."

They heard a loud scream coming from the direction of the restroom.

"Sounds like someone's discovered his body, sugar. I've got a private jet waiting in North Bend. You're welcome to fly away from this messiness. Cops sometimes solve a crime just because life's presented them with a convenient way to solve it."

They exited the restaurant into a waiting limo.

"There must have been some magic in that old silk hat they found," McGrogan sang.

"What happened to him?" she demanded.

"I've ruled out a shellfish allergy because you guys were dining vegan. Other than that, it's up to the men in blue, Bend's finest. I'm sure they'll get to the bottom of it. Good thing you got out of there. Prime suspect and all that. And with your history..."

"My history! My history is unblemished. I was the goodie goodie of Asheville High."

"Oh, you're thinking of Danielle Bond. You're right, lovely girl. Innocent as a kitten. But Renee Bauman, watch out for her. Renee Bauman has the reputation in legal circles as a femme fatale, with emphasis on the fatale. She's wanted in at least two states that I'm aware. The local coppers think she poisoned her boyfriends. I'm starting to detect a pattern, Renee."

"You're a horrible man."

"The worst thing about this job is handling the ingratitude. Must be contagious out here. I don't remember you complaining about anything until the last hour or so. Looked like you enjoyed the little set-up, yes?"

"But you just killed my boyfriend!"

"Not your boyfriend, our client. Maybe it was a shellfish allergy. I've read of a case on a cruise ship where just a waitress walking past with some stuffed shrimp was enough to close the curtain."

"You're a bastard."

"Can't take things personally in this line of work, darling. What do you say we drop you off in Miami? Looks like you can use some R&R. Or would you like to go home for the holidays? Pet the dog, say hello to mom? Take a little nap. You've had a long day. I'll wake you up when the wheels hit the ground."

Between fretting about his disconnection from Barb, enjoying his connection with Devan, playing football, withstanding the rigors of the AP classes, and trying to regain his focus on the saxophone, Oxley had briefly forgotten about McGrogan. But when he walked to Joe's Pizzeria Saturday afternoon, the old man sat waiting in the same booth where he had seen him last. The jukebox was blaring.

"What's your favorite instrumental song? And if you say anything but 'Grazing in the Grass,' you're buying me dinner."

Oxley stared at him mutely.

"This song is a masterpiece. The trumpet, the cowbell.... Wow!!"

"Haven't seen you in a while."

"I've been following you in the papers, my boy. Did that coach of yours suffer a head injury during his playing days? How long was he going to keep you under wraps?"

"He's a great coach."

"Junior, my mom could coach you guys this season. And she'd know enough to hand you the ball thirty or forty times a game. Can you imagine your rushing stats?"

"I like it the way it is. Coaching high school is harder than it looks. The players are kids. Coaches try to do more than just win games."

"Whatever, junior. Have you heard from Alabama yet?"

"I'm hearing from a bunch of schools, but not Alabama."

"Don't worry. And you can bet Nick Saban's not going to run you nine times a game."

"I want to go to school and become a professional musician."

"Okay, let me lay out two alternate scenarios for you. Let's say you even get accepted to Rutgers for music. You go there. Stumble around with a bunch of weirdos like your old girl-friend. Play a bunch of Jazz Messengers bullshit until you get sick of the nursery rhyme quality of those songs and decide you want to play farther out jazz like Ornette Coleman or Archie Shepp and other guys who got bored with the nursery rhyme music. In the process, you make yourself even less employ-able than before, something that barely seems possible. You try to find work after graduation but since jazz is an art form appreciated by about five thousand people worldwide, you end up playing sax in a wedding band to eke out a living while sleeping on friends' couches right on up to your thirties. You pack it in, start giving music lessons to the sons and daughters of your old girlfriend, and hate yourself forever—or you can continue playing football, go to a big D1 superpower, be in the running for the Heisman Trophy, maybe play in the NFL, make a ton of money, sign autographs for money at casinos and car shows afterward. Doesn't seem like much of a choice, if you ask me. But then again, you're the guy who prefers Courtney

Love to the Playboy bunny, so perhaps your judgment is a little skewed."

"I'm enjoying the football stuff. I just like music more."

"As always, junior, it's been my pleasure. Sorry to run out on you, but I've got other stops to make today."

"I'm not your only client?"

"It's like my dear mom used to say, 'there's never just one mouse.'"

Barb and her mom left for Smyrna first thing Sunday morning. They had an 8:30 to 9:30 a.m. appointment for their visit. The visit was limited to an hour. They had to arrive by 8:15. They both needed photo IDs. They could carry no more than five dollars each in currency and their car keys. They left their purses in the trunk of the car. They were searched with a metal detector at the entrance. No property was permitted to be exchanged so Barb could not give her dad a school photo as she hoped. Barb's mom sat in the waiting area. Barb was going to have a half hour alone with her father and then her mom would join them. She was led into the visiting area by a guard and burst into tears. She hugged her dad for a full minute. Her body temperature soared.

"I'm sweating so much that even my back is sweating."

"You look beautiful, honey."

"I have to catch my breath, excuse me."

Barb walked around the small room and leaned against the wall. She cupped her left hand over her mouth and cried.

"Sorry I'm wasting time trying to get myself together."

Her father walked over and held her right hand in both of his hands.

126

"I can't believe you're in here. It feels surreal. I've tried to squash any thoughts I've had of where you are and it's overwhelming to be here. That's why I haven't written lately. I've pretended you were just away somewhere. I don't want you to be here," Barb said.

"Only a while longer, honey."

"I thought you got three to five years. It's been over three years already. Don't they remove some of the time for good behavior?"

"I have to serve the whole five years because there was a handgun involved. I wish I could go back and change things but I can't. I'm really sorry I put you through this. C'mon, do you think we can sit down? I want to hear about your life. Tell me what I'm missing. Think you can compose yourself?"

They sat in plastic chairs with their knees touching.

"I'm really pretty good with the piano. Way better than when you left. I've practiced and practiced and practiced. We still have the piano Mom-Mom left us. I'm hoping I'm good enough to get into the music program at Rutgers in New Brunswick. Because we only have one income and I've had to overcome adversity, I qualify for a special program for promising students from challenging backgrounds. I'm eligible for a bunch of financial aid. I'm eligible for free tutoring when I get there. I'm eligible for a fifth year of financial aid instead of just four years like everyone else."

"So my plan worked! I did this just for you. There really are benefits for sleeping dormitory style with forty other guys for five years and eating canned string beans every night. My kid got extra financial aid!"

"Glad you haven't lost your sense of humor. I was afraid you'd come out shell-shocked."

"I'm fine. I'm on a floor with the older guys. Tell me more about Rutgers."

"Well, I can get in under that special program, but I have to earn my way into the music program and it's competitive as can be. If my audition goes well, I will have an opportunity to study with this amazing jazz pianist, Kenny Barron. He's one of my very favorites. Can you imagine how exciting it will be to be taught by an absolute master? He's recorded on hundreds of albums. Played with Stan Getz, Roy Haynes, Ron Carter, a bunch of geniuses. He's influential. To study with him would be a dream."

"I'm proud of you, honey. You're strong and you're talented and you're smart. When's the audition?"

"In a week."

"You ready?"

"There's been a few bumps but, yes, I'm ready."

"The first thing I'm going to do when I get out is come up to New Brunswick and hear you play. You and Kenny Barron might be playing duets by then. You can give me a command performance."

"Have you been reading?"

"Not much else to do, Barb. I read a lot. There's a library."

"I wish we could all go home together."

"Angel, I'm sorrier than I will ever be able to express. It's been hellish. I will make it up to you for the rest of my life. I never for a moment thought that my actions would separate me from you and Mommy. I repent every single day. I'm going to come out of here a much better man than when I came in. I will be out in 20 months. You'll be finishing your first year of college. New Brunswick's an hour drive from Gloucester. I don't care if you're playing Christmas songs in the dorm lounge, I will be there."

"I wanted to give you some paintings I did but they wouldn't let me bring them into the building. I can't even give you my school picture."

"They don't have the staff to carefully go through things. Too many people come. You can mail them to me. Mommy knows how. What are the paintings of? Do you have a specialty?"

"Dead '60s rock stars."

"What's your masterpiece so far?"

"I have a couple of nice Janis Joplins my teachers like a lot. If the music thing doesn't work out, they think I have the talent to become a commercial artist."

"That's my beautiful girl. So many talents. I'm excited for you. Thank you, honey. I'm really grateful you came to see me. I didn't want you to remember me in this context. I'm reaping what I sowed but I didn't want my little girl to see it. Promise me you'll come visit again after your audition. You can tell me all about it."

"I promise."

They both stood and hugged each other. This time her father cried.

"I apologize for everything, honey. I will make amends, I swear."

"I love you, Daddy. I really miss you. I love you forever."

The drive home was animated.

"I'm so glad I came. I wish I'd come sooner."

"You came at the perfect time. Your dad wasn't ready to face you, and you probably weren't ready to face him. I'm happy it worked out. We'll keep rebuilding from here."

"Daddy called you a 'superstar.'"

"I'm a superstar and I'm gonna go far."

"He's right, though. Thanks for holding it together. You really have."

"We're lucky I had a good education, right? That I'm a nurse. Make sure you finish college. become financially independent."

"In case I marry a drug dealer."

"Don't be smart. Daddy was no more a drug dealer than he's an astronaut. It was a naive fantasy. He was an innocent who thought he could make some easy money."

"I was only kidding. I chose the best parents in the world, didn't I?"

"Just know that we did our best."

When Oxley arrived at school on Monday, his homeroom teacher told him that Coach Claiborn wanted to see him in the athletic director's office.

"Hey, John. You better start stopping down every couple of days to pick up some of this mail. You're getting a half dozen letters a day and it's going to start getting really crazy now. There's an avalanche coming, buddy. Glad you're a good reader. You have anybody that can help you sort out where you want to go with all of this?"

"My mom works a lot and she doesn't know much about sports or college. She'll pretty much leave it up to me."

"Well, if you ever need help or advice, just say so. I'll be happy to help you sort through things. The decision is entirely up to you. This batch of letters is from schools like Colgate, the Ivies, West Chester, Kutztown, Villanova. You've probably already outgrown these places in terms of matching your talent with their level of competition. You might be intrigued by the great education you'll get at some of these places. There's a few Ivy Leaguers who have made it to the NFL, a couple of guys from Villanova. There'd be a lot less wear and tear on your body, too. And some of them might have good music programs. I don't know much about that. Maybe Mr. Bakey and Ms. Bobo in the guidance office could help you with the academic angle, like which schools have good music programs. One school you might find intriguing is Stanford, if they become involved with recruiting you. There's nothing from them yet, but you never know. It's a superior academic school and a great football school. Living in California would be pretty interesting. "

"I'd appreciate any advice or insight that you can give me."

"I think you're lucky in one sense that most other guys aren't: you're able to make this decision on your own because you don't have a bunch of guys trying to live their life through you. Too many guys have a chorus of voices in their ears."

Oxley shoved the envelopes into his backpack.

"Thanks, again."

"John, it's gonna turn into a circus. Trust your gut. It'll never steer you wrong."

"Thanks, Coach. Is it all right if I stay here and write a letter real quick? I only have gym first period."

"Sure. Just sit at that table."

Oxley wrote a note to Barb:

Dear Barb, I'm sorry we've drifted apart. If it's any consolation, I was completely unconscious of having done anything wrong. If I had chance to do it over again, I would have been open and honest about my feelings for you (which have not diminished). I realized a long time ago that I loved you but

I didn't think I needed to express it in any other way than the way I was already expressing it— being respectful, not demanding my own way, being at ease around you, doing activities together, sharing similar likes and dislikes. As you know better than anyone (since you experienced it daily), I have a tendency to remain in my head. I can only feel my body when I turn off my mind. And the way that I've been turning off my thinking and self-consciousness could lead to other problems so I remain skeptical if that is even possible. I'm writing to you because we rehearsed all summer to perform together at the Rutgers admissions audition. Is that still a possibility? Please don't show this letter to anyone."

Love,
Oxley

Oxley carried the note in his back pocket for six periods and finally passed to it a mutual friend at lunch to pass along to Barb. The note resonated and she left Anatomy class crying the following period. That was not the effect he desired, but he was grateful she didn't rip it up or show it to anyone.

Barb was a frequent flyer in the guidance office and never needed a pass or an explanation when she walked through the counseling office doors. Kids like Barbara Gambardello keep guidance offices in business. Computers are used for college searches. Kids can fill out financial aid forms online. Students can apply to colleges online. Letters of recommendation from teachers and coaches can be sent to numerous colleges from central aggregating educational websites. But only a living, breathing guidance counselor can help the Barbara Gambardellos. Barb walked to Ms. Costello's office.

"Are you busy?"

"Never too busy for you, Barb. What's the matter?"

"Oxley is so confusing. He sends mixed signals all of the time. I start to adapt to a 'new normal' and then he does something and I'm immediately knocked off balance."

"We can't put our moods in the hands of other people, even other benevolent people like John Oxley."

"I can't help but be affected by him. I'm tied into him somehow."

"No one is tied into anyone. It's codependency to think you are. You're smart enough to understand that."

"Ahhhhhhhh. I could scream right now I'm so frustrated. And confused."

"You're both in the process of discovering who you are."

"I already know who I am. I wish he'd hurry up and figure it out."

"I remember a girl who just a few weeks ago told me she never wanted to see her dad again. Then a few days ago was walking on air she was so happy to have gone to Delaware to see him. Sound familiar?"

"Yeah."

"So you're not the same person you were a couple of weeks ago. You've grown. You've evolved. And while you are changing and growing and evolving, everyone else is, too. People are dynamic. Life is constantly changing. People are constantly changing. You grew into a bigger person who now has empathy for her dad."

"It's so hard. I feel like I'm further along in gaining an understanding of myself than Oxley is."

"You may be. So you'll have to be patient."

"How can he be so smart and not know what he wants, who he is? And I can't stand that girl Devan."

"It's got nothing to do with being smart. Some very smart people never really figure out who they are. And some people you might think are not smart figure out who they are and are happy."

"Grrrrrrrrrrrrrrrrr."

"You are learning patience, darling. Patience is a pearl of a great price. But if you learn it, watch out! Many blessings will come to you as a result."

The next football opponent was Delsea, a Group 3 perennial sectional championship contender. Gloucester and Delsea have played some classic football game throughout the decades, including one on Thanksgiving Day 1971, when Coach Claiborn quarterbacked the Lions. That game was played in six inches of snow in frigid weather and ended in an 8-8 tie, the only blemish on the Lions' record that season. Today's practice was lively and focused. Nobody had to remind anyone how prominent a victory over Delsea would be. Oxley got a ride home from Mike King when practice ended. Oxley's house had an open outdoor porch to the left of the front door. The house had an inside porch with, improbably, a church pew against the wall. Barb was sitting on the church pew when he entered the enclosed porch. She was pulling her top and bottom lips inside her mouth and biting them. Tears rolled down her cheeks. Oxley unlocked the door to his house and asked, "Do you want to come in?"

Barb walked past him and began to sob. Her face was blotchy and streaked with tears. Oxley sat next to her and held her hand. After what felt like an hour, she caught her breath and began speaking.

"I hate you, Oxley."

Oxley exhaled and remained patient.

"Why? Why didn't you just tell me what your feelings were? Tell me what you were insecure about? Why did we have to go through this emotional torture just to get to this point? We're not arriving at a resolution. We're just arriving at where we would have been if you were open and honest any time in the past, what, two years?"

"I couldn't have articulated my feelings even if I wanted to, Barb. I didn't know what love was. It was only after I didn't have it that I realized that I didn't just like you, I loved you."

"You always treated me like I was your favorite sister. You realize love's a lot deeper than that, right?"

"Yes, I realize it now. But I can't promise that I'm any more capable now than I was then. Ok, I now realize that I live in my head, I don't inhabit my body in any healthy way, I'm afraid of feeling vulnerable, I'm way too self-conscious. But just because I now realize that stuff doesn't magically fix any of them."

"It's hard not to interpret how you acted as some sort of judgment about me. I felt undesirable or else why wouldn't you desire me?"

"I just told you. I did desire you. I do desire you."

"But isn't it up to the partner to make the other partner feel desirable? I'm insecure enough as it is."

"Why can't we just start out as close friends and see where it goes? Why do we have to stay away from each other?"

"I need more than just a buddy, Oxley. Be buddies with someone else. We're not fourteen-year-olds anymore."

"I'm sorry, Barb. But that feels like I'm saying I'm sorry for who I am."

"It's probably intractable. You can't change who you are. I can't change who I am. We want different things from a relationship. Let's just leave it at that. We can be friendly in school. I don't think we should audition together. The trust factor isn't there. Rutgers provides all of the musicians you need for any piece you submit. They'll have someone to play your piano parts. And they'll have someone to play the horn parts for my pieces. It's cleaner that way. Doing it together is impossible for me. I'm sorry."

Barb walked out of his house, hopped into a car, and drove away.

Oxley was stunned. He texted Devan and asked her to meet him at Joe's, neutral territory, hoping it would be easier to resist her charms. He walked to Joe's and found Devan already sitting at the counter.

"Let's sit in a booth," he suggested.

"What's the matter? What happened?"

"When I came home from football, Barb was on my inside porch crying. I really thought she was there to try some sort of reconciliation but, on the contrary, she was there end the whole stupid affair."

"It wasn't much of an affair, to be honest."

"How would you know, Devan? You got here like five weeks ago."

"I don't mean to sound presumptuous, Oxley, but from how you described the dilemma to me in the past, it seems like you two were only compatible as musical partners, not romantic partners. If you want to improve your prospects for romance, you better learn how to become romantic. Ain't no fun trying to coax it out of somebody, trust me. It gets old quick."

"The worst thing is, she doesn't want to do the Rutgers audition with me."

"You're at least as good a musician as she is."

"We rehearsed all summer."

"And all the while, she was waiting for Prince Charming to kiss her. And waiting. And waiting...."

"You're a big help."

"Let me say it in all caps—you and Barb weren't compatible! You're 17! You've got a lot of growing up to do! You can either become one of those men who are always looking for a reason to hang out with their pals, or you can get comfortable feeling vulnerable and being who you are."

"What do I do?"

"Do you really want to go to Rutgers? You can go just about anywhere with playing football."

"I always thought I wanted to be a musician."

"I don't think you really know what you want, Oxley."

"Ahhhhhhhhhh...."

"Why don't you concentrate on football for the next month? See how far you can take the football thing. It's a noble pursuit. Just about everyone in this crazy town is walking taller because of what you guys are accomplishing. And you're the main reason. Take care of what you have the power to take care of. You've got a bunch of big games coming up.

You haven't even gone full throttle yet. Remember that King Arthur story of the sword in the stone? Arthur was the only one able to pull the sword out because he was the only one willing to accept the responsibility of being great, of being the king. Pull the sword out, dude. Become The Man. Give football your full attention. You can figure everything else out after the season ends."

Until now, Oxley had only turned the jets on during the football games. He had tiptoed around at practice, trying not to stand out, going at half speed in any live scrimmaging they did. From this point on, he decided to go full speed in all drills and in all live practice plays. The difference was significant. Hardly any of his teammates could lay a hand on him, let alone wrap him up and tackle him. He deliberately avoided running anyone over but he went full steam every afternoon. His teammates' estimation of him soared. Even the assistant coaches were gape mouthed at times.

He became sullen and withdrawn. Devan began to pick him up after practice every day. They drove to Joe's for dinner and then to her house to complete homework and talk. There were no magic brownies, no new music, no romance. Friday rolled around and the Lions boarded the bus to Delsea. The local sportswriters had chosen the contest as the "Game of the Week." Delsea only had a single loss. The Lions were undefeated. Delsea had played a more challenging schedule. The stands were packed a half hour before the 7 p.m. kickoff. Gloucester High had six fan buses to take students to Franklinville to see the game. Hundreds of other people from Gloucester drove the forty-five minutes to see the game. Dozens of college scouts were in attendance. Oxley did not disappoint.

Delsea drew first blood. They ran the opening kickoff back for a touchdown and kicked the extra point. Oxley had practiced kickoff returns for the first time this week. He was back at the Gloucester goal line to receive the kick. Delsea's coaches had their kicker boot it short to avoid a runback by Oxley, and the Lions took over first and 10 from their own 40-yard line. Oxley was now the starting halfback for the Lions. He took the first handoff and ran around the end and up the sideline for a 60-yard touchdown. He carried for the extra two points. The Lions defense forced Delsea to punt only once the entire first half. The Crusaders possessed a passing game far more effective than anything the Lions had faced yet this season and shredded the Gloucester defense drive after drive. The Lions defense was so porous that making Delsea kick field goals on two possessions felt like a success. On the Gloucester side, Oxley finally showed some vulnerability, fumbling twice. He tripped over one of his lineman's feet the first time and the ball squirted loose before he hit the turf. The second fumble was caused by a blitzing Delsea linebacker who ran unimpeded into Oxley as soon as he took the hand-off. The Lions went into the locker room at halftime down 27-24. As the team came off the field, Gloucester fans shouted their encouragement and support. Then Oxley heard a familiar voice shouting,

"Hold onto the ball, numbnuts. What the hell's the matter with you?"

He glanced over his shoulder to see McGrogan red-faced and screaming, clad in a Alabama Crimson Tide sweatshirt and a baseball cap that read "Karma's a Bitch."

The coaches made defensive adjustments at halftime. Delsea gambled on a fourth and 1 from the Lions 43-yard line and missed a first down by inches. The Lions took over on downs, and three plays later Oxley burst through the Crusader defense for a 50-yard touchdown run. He ran in the two-point conversion, and the Lions led 32-27. The Delsea quarterback made an ill-advised throw on their next possession and a Lions defensive back returned it to the Delsea 20. Oxley caught a screen pass, a new wrinkle in the Gloucester offense, and went 16 yards untouched into the end zone. Gloucester recovered an onside kick, scored immediately, and some Delsea fans began making their way to the stadium exit. The final score was Gloucester 56-Delsea 34. It was the stiffest challenge yet for the Lions. Oxley gained 271 yards on twenty-one carries. They had passed another test and would face the Group 4 Williamstown Braves the following week. On the bus ride home, Oxley received a text from McGrogan. He was unsure how he had gotten his cell number.

"Stop dancing around out there and start running people over like you're capable."

"Who is this?"

"It's McGrogan. You looked like a saxophone player trying to play football rather than an All-State running back."

"I *am* a saxophone player trying to play football. And I think the rushing stats speak for themselves."

"Start running over people. College coaches might start doubting your toughness."

"Ok."

"Roll Tide."

Despite his two fumbles, after the Lions' fifth victory the media spotlight on the Gloucester football team and the intensity of the college recruiting increased tenfold. Gloucester had defeated two top 20 teams, Kingsway and Delsea. Their defense was still questioned in some quarters, but their high-octane offense lad all high schools in South Jersey. They were undefeated through five games for the first time in fifteen years. Sports fans in the town were amped by the Lions' success. They no longer took it for granted. At one time, people assumed that there was something inherently tougher about Gloucester kids and that their kids would prevail on the football field no matter how large, quick, or powerful the opponent. That myth had been dispelled. Toughness only took you so far. This year's Lions team had plenty of tough kids on both sides of the football, but they also were blessed with an alpha athlete at running back who was superior to elite high school players.

Some schools who had been enthusiastically wooing Oxley a few weeks earlier had folded their hands and acknowledged that they were wasting their time pursuing an athlete of his caliber. A few Ivy League schools remained in pursuit with hope that Oxley could be the Calvin Hill of the twenty-first century—a student athlete who gets as much gratification from succeeding in the classroom as in succeeding on the playing field. Villanova remained in pursuit. Brian Westbrook texted Oxley about the advantages of entering the pros with a minimal amount of physical damage inflicted by college opponents. Villanova basketball coach Jay Wright sent Oxley a handwritten letter extolling the virtues of the small Catholic college located just a few miles from Gloucester on Philadelphia's Main Line. All other non-Power conference colleges had dropped out of the race. Oxley had begun to receive letters from SEC, Big 12, Big 10, and PAC 12 coaches. They were form letters at this point but showed that Oxley was beginning to show up on their radar. Rumors flew around Gloucester that Oxley was ready to commit to Notre Dame (the favorite college football team of many Catholics and non-Catholics alike in Gloucester City). Some argued that he should play closer to home at Penn State. Others swore that Nick Saban had Skyped with Oxley at least twice that they were aware of.

Oxley went early to films the next day to catch Coach Claiborn in the trainer's room. It had become a weekly ritual. Oxley arrived even earlier than usual and sat sideways on a second trainer's table because the coach had just begun to ice his knees. He still lifted weights every day. At age sixty-three, he still lifted more weight than the majority of the kids on the high school team. He also stretched every day with a routine that would put most yoga teachers to shame. He had maintained his exact college workout routine every day for the past forty-one years.

"Nice to pick up another W, hey buddy?"

"Yes. Sorry about the fumbles."

"They happen. You see fumbles in college games and in the pros. Tighten your focus on hanging onto the football, that's all. No big deal."

"I'm glad we won."

"Yeah, me too," he laughed.

"Williamstown is good?"

"Williamstown is always good. You ever see their high school? It's a big as the Deptford Mall. They ought to be good. They have kids who don't start for them but would start for darn near anybody else in the conference. It's going to be a challenge."

"At least we're healthy and we have Jackson coming back. That'll help."

"Jeff coming back is going to help. He'll be back at defensive back. We missed him. So we are going to be better this week than last week and that's good. Jeff won't be playing offense any more. We'll try to protect that knee."

"Good."

"Your life is going to keep getting more and more complicated, buddy. We've had a bunch of calls from college coaches asking what time we practice and where we practice. Naturally, the college guys can't get to our games on most Fridays because they play on Saturday. A few have been in the stands if they had a bye week. But you've probably outgrown most of the schools who have already been here. Now the big-time football schools are curious enough to have a look at you. I doubt we'll see any head coaches, but we're going to see their assistants. Colleges don't throw scholarship offers at people unless they think you can play at their level. Sometimes the D3s are looking for bodies, prospects, kids who might pan out but might not pan out. They're looking to fill the dormitories with students. The college is glad that the football coaches are adding to their enrollment and the coaches hope that certain guys are legitimate players. D2s are pickier because they are offering you scholarship money. The pressure is more intense to pick the right guys. These guys earn a living and feed their families by winning. Think about that. If your team loses for a couple of years, your family finances are at serious risk. That's real pressure. D1 coaching is all about producing winning teams, period. If you lose, alumni pressure the college to get rid of you. People are going to start blowing smoke at you. Everyone you meet is going to have advice about what you should do, where you should go. I know. I went through it. And you're a pretty reserved guy just like me. You don't like people all that much to begin with."

"You have any advice?"

"Stick with the people who have been supporting you before any of this happened. People who were by your side when you were just another kid in Algebra class. You still go out with that band girl with the purple hair?"

"We never really went out romantically, but we hung out all the time."

"The girl with the glasses, right? I just assumed she was your girlfriend."

"Yes, but we aren't speaking at the moment. We had a disagreement."

"That's too bad. She's someone you trusted a lot, right?"

"She was, yes. But I've got a new friend now. I trust her."

"Eh. I don't always like the new friends. You're going to have plenty of people who wouldn't give you the time of day when you were on the JV team wanting to get closer to you now that you have a certain shine to you. You're the exact same kid who was with us last year. Where were these folks then?"

"Well, this new girl just moved here at the end of the summer. She's from Florida."

"She's not telling you to sign with the Florida Gators, is she? Maybe she was sent here on a mission," he smiled.

"No. She's not offering any advice except to keep my focus on football."

"Well, I think I like her already."

After films, Oxley decided to walk home to try to clear his head. Cars routinely honked to him now. People he knew, people he didn't know, people he would never know. Nearly everyone he passed on the street said hello. He wasn't long for this town, but it had been good for him. The town did him a favor by leaving him alone for seventeen years. Now it was trying to do him another favor by paying attention to him.

The audition numbers for Rutgers were so complex and intricate that they needed hours of daily practice. A saxophone is relatively easy to play but extremely difficult to master. Oxley had worked years and years developing the embouchure and mastering the fingerings to more challenging jazz pieces. Certain rhythms, intonations, and accidentals required daily, intense practice. It was what had distinguished Oxley from the thousands of other high school sax players—thousands of hours of practice. He became serious about the instrument as a fourteen-year-old freshman. Now that he was losing himself in football, he was less committed to life as a musician. He wondered what it meant to change his mind, to change his career aspirations so quickly. Was he ever truly committed to music? Or was he more committed to his bond with Barb?

He texted Devan and asked her to meet him at Joe's. He was starving. He walked past his house, down Brown Street to Mercer, turned left and walked to Broadway. By the time he arrived, Devan was pulling up in her Jetta.

"How were films?"

"Good, except I had to watch the two fumbles a couple of times. One was preventable, one was bad luck. I'll be more aware and careful. I'm just learning how to play running back."

"Were the coaches mad?"

"They were happy we won. They were way more concerned by our pass defense than the fumbles. The coaches are smart. We've been working on our own passing game so much every week and still haven't unveiled it. It's pretty good, too."

"What, in case you get hurt?"

"In case a team stops our running game."

"Highly doubtful."

"Anyway, I have to figure out what I'm going to do about the audition at Rutgers because I've been slacking as far as rehearsing. I couldn't pass an audition today. If I have any hope of passing it Friday, I've almost got to devote the rest of today, all of tomorrow, and then a few hours Monday through Thursday nights. The audition is scheduled for Friday."

"Have you talked to Barb? Weren't you two planning on auditioning together? Have you told her of your recent noncommitment to music? You wouldn't want to screw things up for her."

"She cut me loose and told me she didn't want to see me anymore. She didn't trust me. Correctly, as it's turned out. She has good intuition."

"That's because she's a witch."

"I miss her."

"You miss her? Or did the ten percent of your emotional energy you use to give her just flare up again? You need to keep working on yourself. She can't help you figure out what to do and neither can anyone else. You have to do it alone. And since you keep all emotions as far from consciousness as possible, you have this constant stalemate about what to do. You want my advice?"

"Not really?"

"Then why'd you text me?"

"Guess at the time I wanted your advice."

"That was like ten minutes ago."

"Ok, what's your advice, wise one?"

"Action talks and bullshit walks, that's my advice. If you really wanted to play the sax professionally, you'd practice all the time. People change what they want to do all the time. Kids want to be police officers, firemen, doctors, veterinarians, professional athletes, ballet dancers…. But at some point, the reality of their situation becomes apparent: they aren't brave enough, talented enough, dedicated enough, don't have the perseverance to get through the preliminaries. Life sorts itself out and people become what they were destined to become, what they were created to become. The people meant to be doctors become doctors. The people meant to become ballet dancers become ballet dancers. The people who weren't meant to separate and become something else—something they were meant to become all along. Your actions have been talking ever since I met you. Playing the sax provided many benefits but is an imprudent way for you—John Oxley—to make a living. So your spirit led you in another direction, toward different opportunities, neither better or worse in any qualitative way but better for your spirit. If you weren't meant to play football, why have you mysteriously become so good at it?"

"It's a long story."

"We all have long stories, Oxley. Your story's no longer than anyone else's."

"Should I ask the guidance counselor to notify Rutgers that I won't be auditioning?"

"Action talks, bullshit walks. Your actions these past weeks leading up to a critical audition indicate that maybe you are not as committed to becoming a jazz musician as you thought. It's no different than another boy figuring out he doesn't really want to be a fireman. Don't put too fine a point on it. You've evolved in another direction just like the kid who used to dream about fighting fires."

"Darn. All those hours of practicing!"

"Don't get melodramatic. You didn't lose your skills. With further commitment, you'd become better than ever and you are pretty damned good already. You have the skill, you didn't have the will."

"It's a crossroad where I'm taking one path rather than another."

"There's plenty of other paths. Don't pretend there's only two."

Oxley was featured on a website called 24/7Sports Composite's recruit rankings as the fiftieth best high school running back in the nation. Videos of his touchdown runs made the Hudl Highlights video mix on YouTube. It received thousands of views over the weekend. Colleges called Coach Claiborn to set up recruiting visits after the high school season ended on Thanksgiving. Younger kids knocked on his front door asking for an autograph. The coaches put in plays to get Oxley the ball through pitchouts, reverses, and screen passes. They anticipated that opponents would send their linebackers in directly at Oxley for the next few weeks. Many new wrinkles were put in for the Williamstown game. The Lions' playbook had evolved since the season opener six weeks before. The Williamstown game would be a test of the Lions mettle.

They rode in silence down Route 42. Their athletic trainer had decided on Wednesday day that Jeff Jackson needed another week without contact to recover from his knee injury. This left Gloucester once again vulnerable to a passing attack. Williamstown threw the ball so many times the first half that the twenty-four minutes of game clock took an hour and twenty minutes to complete. Their quarterback, a highly touted sophomore already drawing interest from college recruiters, finished the half completing fourteen of twenty-one passes for 203 yards and two touchdowns. The Braves had run in for another score and took a 23-16 lead into the locker room. Oxley rushed for 142 yards and two touchdowns at this point but Williamstown had a lopsided time-of-possession advantage that kept him off the playing field.

Gloucester bobbled the second-half kickoff and started play from their own 12-yard line. They faked a handoff to Oxley on second down and completed their first touchdown pass of the season, an 81-yarder to tight end Mike King. Oxley rushed for the two-point conversion and the Lions led by a point. The Braves came right back, eating up five minutes of the clock with a series of short passes and runs off tackle, and scoring on a quarterback sneak from the 2. Williamstown led 30-24. The Braves kicked off and Oxley returned it across the 50. Three plays later, Lions quarterback Denny Miller found King all alone down the right sideline, and the third quarter ended with the Lions leading 32-30.

Williamstown mounted another long drive but turned the ball over inside the Lions 20 on an interception that caromed off the hands of a Braves wide receiver into the hands of a Gloucester linebacker. The Braves seemed disheartened and Oxley caught a screen pass on first down and ran 81 yards into the end zone. After the conversion, Gloucester led 40-30. Williamstown would not quit. They picked up a succession of first downs and found the end zone on a 40-yard passing strike, cutting the Gloucester lead to three points, with less than a minute to go. The Braves recovered an onside kick, picked up a first down but missed a game-tying field goal attempt with only seconds left to secure the Lions hard-fought 40-37 victory.

Gloucester had navigated the most challenging parts of their schedule and remained undefeated at 6-0. They would play two Group 1 schools, Penn Grove and Salem, before the Thanksgiving Day classic against rival Gloucester Catholic. The Lions knelt on one knee in the end zone and listened to Coach Claiborn:

"Great effort. This was another character test. You learn way more from these games than you do the easier ones. We beat a very good football team but all of us—coaches and players—can look back on plays where we should have been smarter. Remember those plays when you go home tonight. Write yourselves a message if you have to as a reminder to read before next week's game. What could you have done that would have helped us? We all have lots of room for improvement. And the only football opponent I want to hear mentioned this week is Penn Grove. We are a Group 1 school still climbing back from a ditch we drove into. We aren't good enough to overlook anybody. Respect our opponents. People around town are going to start talking to you about Thanksgiving. Let it fall on deaf ears. I respect Penns Grove enough that I will be studying their game tapes as soon as I can and as often as I can. You better respect them or they will beat us. We've got a big bullseye drawn on our backs at this point. It's going to make the season of any team that can beat us. So if you don't want the Penns Grove guys to be sitting at their class reunion twenty-five years from now reminiscing about how they upset Gloucester, don't waste a minute this week thinking of any team other than Penn Grove. Take care of the present, and the future will take care of itself."

The Gloucester fans waited and congratulated the players as they got onto the bus. The bus ride home was quieter than normal. No one on the team thought they were invincible and giving up 37 points highlighted that fact. Getting back Jeff Jackson would be a big help but there was no guarantee that he was coming back. "Still week to week," was how the trainer put it. Oxley texted Devan that he was tired and would see her tomorrow after films. He saw on Facebook that Barb had heard from Rutgers:

"Today is the happiest day of my life. I've been notified that I passed my audition and have been accepted into the Mason Gross School of Performing Arts at Rutgers. Can't believe I will be learning piano from my idol, Kenny Barron. So happy!!!"

Oxley was happy and relieved that he hadn't harmed her chances in any way. He was happy for Barb. He thought about texting her his congratulations but couldn't stand the rejection if she texted back something snarky or didn't respond. Even if she simply said "thanks," it'd be too dramatic a comedown from the heights of their friendship.

When the team bus got back to Gloucester, the boys headed into the locker room to put back their equipment. Oxley lingered a minute to talk with Jeff Jackson and when he left, everyone was gone from the parking lot. Mike King must have assumed Oxley was getting a ride from Devan. Oxley thought of texting Devan for a ride but decided to walk home and clear his head. The pressure was mounting from all sides. So many people were invested in the idea that that a rejuvenated team meant a rejuvenated town. The Lions' winning streak had undoubtedly raised the mood of Gloucester High School and Gloucester City. It wasn't only the players who were walking taller.

The town was shrouded in a clear sky, late autumn darkness. Many of the houses that Oxley passed were decorated for Halloween. Pumpkins, skeletons, ghouls, and goblins stared from many of the doorways. The air was crisp, and Oxley walked home in the cutoff t-shirt he wore under his shoulder pads. He regretted missing his ride. When he turned the corner at Greenwood, he began to jog. He wanted to raise his body temperature. He jogged past a lake known as the Minnow Hole, crossed the street, jogged past Martin's Lake and felt the familiar flush of warmth that exercise brings. He jogged another block and resumed walking when he crossed Somerset Street toward Monmouth. He continued along Johnson Boulevard toward Hudson when he noticed someone walking along the railroad tracks across the street, singing,

"Send the freshmen out for gin,
And don't let a sober sophomore in…"

The singing stopped briefly as the guy struggled to remember the lyrics:

> *"We never stagger, we never fall,*
> *We sober up on wood alcohol…"*

It was McGrogan, walking parallel to Oxley down Johnson. He was wearing an Alabama Crimson Tide hoodie with a large red elephant on the front. He wore a baseball cap that read "Karma's a Bitch." He seemed oblivious to Oxley's presence.

> *"And when we yell,*
> *We yell like hell,*
> *For the glory of Gloucester High. Go Lions!"*

Oxley marveled at the guy's craziness.

"You all right over there?"

McGrogan stopped dramatically and stared across Johnson Boulevard.

"Who goes there, mate?"

Oxley took a few steps into the street, and McGrogan walked tentatively up the hill that leads to the railroad tracks from the street.

"Why if it isn't my old friend, Herschel Walker!"

Oxley waited until McGrogan met him in the middle of Johnson Boulevard and they walked together back to the sidewalk on the western side off the boulevard. McGrogan had a devilish glint in his eye.

"Were you at the game, McGrogan?"

"Yes, I was. Do they still give out postseason awards for Unsung Hero and stuff like that?"

"Yes."

"I'm nominating your quarterback. What's his name?"

"Dennis Miller."

"He is damn good, brother."

"I know."

"Have you signed with Alabama yet?"

"Don't think they've sent me anything."

"Don't worry, they will. Nick Saban does not let the grass grow under his feet. That's what makes him Nick Saban. He's probably talking about you right now. I put a little bug in his ear."

"I'm sure you have a lot of pull with Nick Saban."

They turned on Gaunt Street and walked up the hill to Brown.

"Son, you're all over social media. You're a YouTube sensation. You're getting thousands of views every day. Every Cub Scout in Wyoming knows who you are, so Nick Saban definitely knows who you are."

"I'm letting my coach handle all of the recruiting mail. He's sifting through it and we're going to sit down after the season and prioritize the schools I'm interested in. I don't have time for recruiting visits until after the season ends on Thanksgiving, anyway. It was becoming a distraction."

"A distraction for who, you or your coach? Because most kids get excited about all of the recruiting attention."

"I'm not like most kids."

"Right, I forgot. How did that Rutgers audition go? Did they like the Sonny and Cher act that you and the girl cooked up?"

"I didn't go. Barb went. She got in."

"Ohhh. You didn't go to the audition? I guess that puts a little bit more pressure on the football thing, doesn't it?"

"Somewhat. Not enough to sell my soul though."

Oxley walked up the steps of his house and said, "I'll be right out. I need a hoodie. It's chilly."

"You're not inviting me in?"

Oxley came right out pulling a Lions hoodie over his head. He pulled a ski cap out of the front pocket. Oxley sat in a double-wide swing that his mom had inherited from her grandmom, and McGrogan sat in a faded Adirondack chair on Oxley's front porch.

"So tell me what your options are, now that you passed on the saxophone audition? Community college with all of the other baton twirlers? You're probably better at the sax than some the music professors. Sounds like a waste of your time. Meanwhile, Lady Gaga soars to new heights at a real college music program with real musicians as instructors. Maybe she'll give you a call some day for a gig if her first seven choices of a sax player can't make it that day. If it's for a wedding reception and the guests get drunk enough, maybe you two can do a rendition of 'I Got You, Babe,' but with no vocals—just saxophone honks and tinkles of the piano. I know I'd pay to see it."

"I don't know how long I want to commit to the football thing. The hundred days is fine, but after that I'm thinking I might want my life back."

"And I bet your mother has accused you on a number of occasions of being ungrateful. Just ten weeks ago, you were the invisible man. People who passed you on the street, kids who passed you in the hallways, they didn't even see you. You were a nobody. Half the teachers at your high school probably didn't know who you were. Now everybody knows you. Cars honk at you. People stare out their window if they happen to notice you. Girlfriend-wise, you've traded up from a faded Volkswagen bus with no heat, cassettes all over the floor, and unlit incense sticks, to a 2017 VW sports car with every innovation. If you give it up, where is that going to leave you? It's going to be even more fun at the college level. Better girls, better cars, even more acclaim…."

"How am I going to retain the football skills if the West Coast guy gets reinstated?"

"There's always another maniac doing something maniacal. Why do you think some guys switch positions when they get to college. Hell, there's quarterbacks who have become linemen or linebackers. It's a shell game with this karma thing, and I'm a master magician."

"I'm not sure if I can trust you. I got no guarantee at all beyond the hundred days."

"Junior, you just hurt my feelings. Do you realize I was named 'Most Dependable' in my high school yearbook? Haven't I come through big time for you? Didn't this entire scenario seem completely implausible? Yet I made it happen!"

"What I like about the football stuff is seeing so many people happy. The other guys on the team are great people. The coaches are great. I love seeing the people around Gloucester smiling again, dreaming of beating Gloucester Catholic. But does the success make me feel any better about myself? No."

"Maybe you have a mood disorder. I know a guy who gives electroshock treatment completely off the books. He used to be a doctor but got into a jam with the insurance industry so now he practices down his basement. He swears the electroshock works wonders for depression, and I think you'd be a good candidate."

"My mood is my mood. It's who I am. Unexcitable."

"Unexcitable or unexciting? You used to be both."

"You're big on 'scenarios.' Give me the scenarios if I sign on for another hundred days and if I don't."

"No, no, no, no, no. The trial period is one hundred days. The signature means you're signing on for the duration."

"Duration of what?"

"Duration of your life, junior. I've got a lot invested in you. You'll be college football sensation, that much I will guarantee. All the applause, all the parades, etcetera, etcetera. After that we'll have a little tête-à-tête and see where we want to go from there. Maybe the NFL, maybe you get back into music, maybe politics. We'll be partners. Your life will never be boring again. People like Barb will seem like nightmares from your youth— insignificant, ditzy, and dull. From now on, you'll get it right."

"What's the scenario if I don't sign the contract? If I want to steer my own life?"

"That's where the rubber hits the road, jawbone. For one, you'll be left with your own meager JV-level skills for the

Gloucester Catholic game. You will have negative rushing yards against the Rams. You'll be the laughing stock of South Jersey. And the video of your 'highlights' from that game? Every Gloucester Catholic fan across the state will watch it a thousand times, admiring how the mighty Rams stuffed the great John Oxley. It might break the YouTube record for views."

"What??"

"Yeah, the hundred days ends at ten fifteen Thanksgiving morning. You never looked at the calendar? One hundred days is one hundred days. The contract went into effect August 16 at ten thirty. Imagine playing Gloucester Catholic, with the hopes of every working stiff in Gloucester riding on your back, every carpenter, every teacher, every electrician, every plumber, the ladies in the cafeteria, everybody hoping that just this once the little guy might slay the giant, and you stumbling, fumbling, tripping over your own two feet. People will want to hang you. You might have been invisible before football but you weren't a social leper. I don't even think Buffalo Barb would talk to you. Oh, that's right. She already doesn't talk to you! And if you think a grifter like the chick in the Jetta is going to stick by your side, you're dreaming. I can promise you right now she isn't."

"Noooooooo."

"Yesssssssss."

Oxley groaned and threw his head back. McGrogan continued:

"Is there an online high school you can finish the year with? Then maybe you can join the service and asked to get shipped to a war zone right after boot camp. You're going to need something that dramatic—people trying to shoot your balls off—to forget about your colossal failure."

Oxley sat in silence.

"You've still got couple of weeks to ponder it, sonny. Stay focused. Let's go into the big Thanksgiving showdown undefeated. Imagine how hyped that game will be. You know the Rams will be undefeated. Hell, they're always undefeated."

"Get out of here, will you?"

McGrogan got up, tipped his cap toward Oxley, and headed down Hudson Street toward Johnson Boulevard.

He started singing the Gloucester Catholic alma mater:

"We hail thee Gloucester Catholic,
Thy honor and glory proclaim..."

The next morning Oxley spoke with Coach Claiborn.

"Hey Coach."

"Hey, John. Good one last night, right?"

"Pretty crazy toward the end."

"I think the best you can hope for any team, in a nine-game season, is three great games, three decent games, and three games where not everything goes right. Every game reveals something, but sometimes the ones where things don't go right really draws stuff out of people. Like Miller and Kingy last night. If our defense stopped them a few more times, we'd probably have just kept running the ball. But people were forced to step up and those guys really came through. Quality people. People you can feel confident leading the charge when they have to."

"Those guys were great."

"How are you feeling?"

"Things are good. I'm glad we have a good passing game. Never know when we might need it again."

"You trying to tell me something, dude?"

"No, no, just better safe than sorry."

"We've been practicing the passing game every day since day one, you know that. You never know what might happen. Look at Jeff Jackson. We really counted on him and he ends up being injured for most of the season. First thing you earn about coaching: You always need a plan B."

"Cool."

"Cool? You are one-of-a-kind buddy. You're going to have a mountain of letters to sift through once the season ends. You might be the most recruited, least interested athlete in Gloucester history. Why don't you let me give you a pile of ones I think would be a good fit for you and you can read them at night or when you're bored? You leaning any certain way?"

"Tell you the truth, I'm leaning toward not playing any more after we beat Gloucester Catholic."

"You serious? Better think that one over, buddy. Wait until after the season. It will feel like some of the pressure's off. People will wait for you. The season wears us out mentally. You'll feel rejuvenated by mid-December. You might even start feeling bored without all the adrenaline rush you get during the season. Keep your thoughts to yourself for a while. Keep your own counsel. The answer will come to you. Don't put any pressure on yourself one way or the other."

"You wouldn't be disappointed?"

"What, if you didn't play in college? No, I wouldn't be disappointed. You do what's best for you and I will stand by you. You don't need my approval, that's for sure. You will have my approval no matter what your decision is."

"Thanks, Coach."

"John, we all do as much as we can handle. Some guys can work on fixing stuff around their house all day long. I try it for about ten minutes and I'm so frustrated I want to smash the hammer into the wall. Ten minutes is all I can handle. On the other hand, I can be patient as can be with you guys. During the season I get here about six o'clock in the morning and leave about ten at night. It doesn't bother me at all. But I've got every contractor in town on speed dial because I can't handle the smallest project without having a breakdown. We all do as much as we can do. You don't owe me or anybody else a thing."

Practice that week centered around fine tuning the passing game. The Williamstown game showed the value and the foresight of tweaking the passing attack and making it efficient and reliable. Quarterback Denny Miller had demonstrated poise and deftness. Gloucester's coach had made a lifetime study of the position. He had worked with Miller all summer long, assuming that the Lions offense would center around his strong arm and agility in the pocket. The Lions sophomore wide receivers also demonstrated great growth. Oxley's emergence as a premier running back put the passing game on the back burner, but the team had devoted as much time on their passing attack as on their running attack.

Penn Grove was a Group 1 school in Salem County that had won the South Jersey Group 1 state sectional championship in 2012, finishing that season with a perfect 12-0 record and setting a state single season scoring record with 621 points. Like most Group 1 schools, the loss of a few key athletes to graduation changed the school's fortunes and the Red Devils had struggled this season. They only had two wins and were playing without much enthusiasm heading into the final weeks of the season. The game was a laugher. Gloucester led 32-0 at halftime. Oxley had gained 199 yards rushing by the half. The Lions didn't throw the ball once. The JVs played the entire second half, and Gloucester left with a 40-12 victory. There was only Salem and Gloucester Catholic standing between the Lions and a perfect season. Coach Claiborn spoke to the boys after the victory:

"Good game today. I'm happy that we didn't take anything for granted and we came right out and executed from the start. I appreciate how you guys haven't underestimated anyone. Good teams take care of business. Pep rallies and stuff like that are for the fans and the cheerleaders. Whether you think you played well today or if you feel short of your expectations, we won. That's all that matters. Our next opponent is the Salem Rams. They are the only Rams that I want any of you guys talking about and thinking about this week. Other people, people who are not going out onto the battlefield with us every week, they are going to look past Salem and start talking and talking and talking about Gloucester Catholic. If we want to go into the Gloucester Catholic game undefeated, we better not think about them until this time next week. Salem is capable of kicking our ass if we are distracted. Keep your eyes on the prize. The prize this coming week is how satisfying it's going to be doing everything we can to prepare for Salem, focusing exclusively on beating Salem, and then executing our game plan as efficiently as possible next Friday night against the Salem Rams. Anybody who brings up any other team, respectfully ignore them. First things first. Great effort tonight. See you at films tomorrow."

Oxley texted Devan after getting of the team bus back in Gloucester but never heard back from her. She had become increasingly withdrawn and remote. Oxley had no reason to expect her to be available at his beck and call. She wasn't his type, and they both realized that. Oxley talked with her many times about his regrets about not seeing Barb. Devan realized that Oxley was in love with someone else but had become his best friend and confidant. After films on Saturday, Oxley texted her again.

"Where you been, old bean?"

"I'm a mess. The wheels are about to come off."

"What's that mean?"

"There's so much I can't tell you, Oxley. How I got here. Where I came from. My history. My dismal future."

"Your dismal future? You look like a Kardashian. You're wise about the world."

"I'm world weary, not world wise."

"I don't understand at all. Can we hang out? Come to my house. No one's home until real late. We can hang out."

"If anyone could understand, it would be you. If I feel any better later, I'll text."

"Just don't do anything harmful. I'll come sit with you. We don't even have to talk."

"Thanks, Oxley."

Oxley texted her again on Sunday, but Devan didn't text back. She wasn't in school on Monday.

Joe's closes at 8 p.m. At 7:55 p.m., Devan went back to the restaurant and sat at the counter. Nick had the lights dimmed and was cleaning the grill.

"You know we close in five minutes, right?"

"Hi, Nick. Can I talk to you? I'm Oxley's friend."

"Talk to me *right now*?"

"Yes, do you have kids you have to get home to or any obligations?"

"Are you ok?"

"No."

"Let me lock the door and turn off the lights in the back."

"Thanks. I have no one to talk to."

"How about Oxley or your mom? I'm not exactly the Dear Abby type, you might have noticed."

"I don't have a mom, Nick. I do, but she's not around here."

"Who do you live with? How do you afford that nice car, if you don't mind me asking?"

"My life is a ruse. You know that guy with the Alabama hoodie that comes in here once in a while to talk with Oxley? He's a bad, bad man. I met him a few years ago because I was naive and innocent and foolish. I made a deal with him that I thought provided me with all these benefits, but it's led me here now, desperately pleading for help."

"I knew that guy had a bad vibe the minute I saw him. I know it sounds weird, but when he walks under the fluorescent lights, they flicker. I noticed it the first time he was in here and I paid attention every time since. The lights never flicker when anyone else passes under them and they flicker every time he does. And my sister-in-law who works here said the guy gives her the creeps."

"Oxley's in so far over his head. He is a puppy. That guy McGrogan is a voracious dragon. Oxley's life is in grave danger. My life is over. McGrogan knows everything we do. He senses quickly if you even think of betraying him."

"How did you ever meet the guy? "

"I was a dumb eighteen-year-old, just out of high school, wishing I was prettier, more popular, all the silly stuff girls worry about in high school."

"Hard to believe you didn't realize you were pretty."

"I didn't look like this then. I was as plain Jane as you can get. McGrogan appealed to my vanity and my insecurity. He senses those things in others. He transformed me into this physical body but he stole my soul. McGrogan made all of these superficial promises to me. I'd have nice clothes, nice furniture, nice things. What I don't have is free will. I don't get to choose where I live. I can only date the operation target, in this case, Oxley. I'm a pawn in a game and always expendable if I don't cooperate. McGrogan doesn't give second chances. He will somehow intuit that I am being disloyal. My life is in serious jeopardy. He's going to make me disappear one way or another."

"What's this have to do with Oxley?" Nick asked.

"Oxley made the same deal with the same devil. McGrogan is telepathic. He realized that Oxley harbored a secret ambition and he exploited his human frailty, just like he exploited mine. He gave Oxley the strength, agility, and athleticism to do what he's done on the football field. It's the same contract as mine. One hundred days. The one hundred-day mark is Thanksgiving morning at ten thirty. If Oxley doesn't sign that contract, I guarantee you will never see him again. He was a pawn in a game, and McGrogan's already squeezed everything he needed from Oxley. I don't see how McGrogan can ever use him again. Oxley's an awkward, introverted geek. Not a lot of demand for those types for the kind of mischief McGrogan makes. Oxley's days are numbered."

"How long do we have?"

"McGrogan will eliminate Oxley on Thanksgiving if he doesn't sign the contract. Or he'll soon spirit him away from here and eliminate him. Either way, Oxley's doomed."

"Good thing McGrogan's operating in Gloucester."

"What difference does that make?"

"Gloucester's not like anywhere else."

"McGrogan is a powerful, evil force. Don't be put off by that clown act of his. He will char you into embers in the blink of an eye. I've seen what he can do. He is a malevolent force."

"Can he breathe underwater?"

"All I know is that he has no conscience, zero empathy, and he's ruthless. He also possesses powers that are not of this earth."

"There's three ways of doing things—the right way, the wrong way, and *the Gloucester way*."

"What the heck does that mean?"

"It means I don't think McGrogan's ever been to Gloucester before."

At the film session on Saturday, the team watched films of Salem. Every other week, they had reviewed the film of the previous night's game but there wasn't much to be gleaned from watching the blowout of Penn Grove. The coaches wanted everyone to see for themselves how dangerous Salem was. Salem was 6-1 on the season. They had sent all kinds of players to college and the great Anthony "A.B." Brown to the NFL. The current Salem running back, Todd Bell, had recently committed to Wisconsin. They were athletic and confident. The Gloucester coaches called it a "trap game," meaning a game where a lack of focus would result in a loss. Partisans debated online all week who was a better running back—Bell or Oxley. Fans of Salem claimed Gloucester was a one-man team, and fans of Gloucester said the same thing about Salem. The local sportswriters wrote feature stories on both of them. The *Philadelphia Inquirer* selected the contest as their "Game of the Week." Oxley was walking to Mike King's car after practice on Tuesday when he noticed the red Jetta. He told King he'd see him tomorrow and found Devan smiling at him as he approached. She rolled down her window.

"Do you want a ride?"

"Sure."

When they pulled out of the high school parking lot, Oxley asked, "Are you feeling better?"

"I had to figure something out. It's a tough one and I don't want to talk about it. Once I made a decision, I felt lighter. It's a situation where there isn't any easy path. I felt like I was out of bullets but still involved in a shootout. I didn't know what to do. I needed some time by myself and I needed to draw upon my own resources. Sorry if I ignored you."

"No need to be sorry. Did you figure something out?"

"I discovered I still had one bullet left in the chamber."

"Did you use it?"

"I will when I need to. Let's go get stoned."

"I gotta stay focused."

"Oxley, how do you exist on so little fun every day? You should become a monk. It's probably hard for guys who enjoy the secular world to drop everything and take those vows of chastity, poverty, and obedience. But you already adhere to them. It would only be moving to new quarters and continuing to live the way you already live."

"I have plenty of fun."

"You're a deadhead, Oxley. Face it and embrace it."

"Whatever I am, I'm hungry. Can we get something to eat?"

"Sure. Joe's?"

"Where else?"

"You're so cute, Oxley. Your entire universe consists of your house, Gloucester High, The PAL Club, Joe's Pizzeria, wherever the football team bus drops you off every other week to play football.... And you seem content to keep it that way. Ever think you might venture out into the wider world one day?"

"I'm going to, just wait and see."

"And, of course, I won't mention that you've been in love with the same girl since, what, fourth grade or so?"

"You're hilarious."

"But since you never got around to telling her or showing her, she moved on. However, I have it on quality intel that she might be having second thoughts about the little drummer boy and that she might call the whole thing off. Still have feelings for her?"

"Always."

They arrived at Joe's and went inside, appreciating the warm respite from the November cold.

"You know what's ironic, Dev? You're a slacker at school but smart about life."

"I earned any wisdom the hard way. The very hard way."

"What do you think you'll do in life?"

"That's enough about me, doctor. Let's talk about you. You may not have access to this great fount of wisdom much longer. It's close to that time."

"What time is that?"

"I'm splitting this scene soon, Oxley. I've got promises to keep. Promises I made to myself."

"How soon?"

"Soon as I know my beautiful boy Oxley is going to be all right."

"I am grateful for you, Devan, but I'm gonna be all right. No need to worry."

"I'd be worrying a lot less if you'd start worrying a little more. You're a baby lamb that's wandered into the wolf's woods. Saxophone players just don't wake up one day and find out that they never realized that they were actually a world class athlete. And none of their coaches ever noticed that either. Or their gym teachers. Or their friends. Sooner or later, the bill comes due."

"You're losing me, Devan."

"No. *You're* losing you. I'm trying to help you find yourself. Ever hear about the guy who brought a knife to a gun fight? In your case, it's a butter knife."

"I feel like I'm in one of those kung fu movies where the warrior listens to the holy man in the cave."

"Let's eat, grasshopper. That's enough wisdom for one day. Go play a few of those musty old songs. Here's a quarter."

Oxley walked over to the jukebox and played "Little Bit O'Soul" by the Music Explosion, "Born on the Bayou" by Creedence Clearwater Revival, "The Warmth of the Sun" by the Beach Boys, "Magic Carpet Ride" by Steppenwolf, "There's a Place" by The Beatles, and "Laugh, Laugh" by the Beau Brummels. They ate in silence listening to the music.

"Did any of these bands have a drummer, Oxley?"

"You're so used to drum machines, Devan, you can't even hear when an actual person is keeping the beat."

"What beat? These songs don't have beats," she laughed.

"You're used to machines making music. You can't get used to people making music."

Football practice was quieter and more focused Wednesday and Thursday. The players were sullen and withdrawn, even in school. The only players who appeared lighthearted in school this week were the kids who had no chance of playing against Salem. The kids who would see action Friday evening felt the pressure of responsibility. It was difficult to find anything to distract themselves from the pressure. Video games were played with less enthusiasm and spirit. Many of them studied football videos on Hudl all week. They couldn't wait until game time to actually get into motion and fight the battle.

Friday rolled around and John A. Lynch Field was filled a half hour before kickoff. The game lived up to its hype. The Lions kicked off and both teams got on the scoreboard early. The Lions couldn't contain Bell, and Salem couldn't stop Oxley. The first quarter came to a close with the score tied at 14 and with the Lions deep in Salem territory. Lightning struck for Salem when Bell intercepted a pass inside the 5 and returned it 95 yards untouched for a Salem touchdown. The Lions had attempted two passes. One was an incomplete pass on a two-point conversion and the other was a pick six for

Salem. Gloucester took the lead for the first time when Oxley sprinted 60 yards up the sideline and also cashed in on a two-point conversion. The Lions led 22-21.

Salem came right back on a series of runs by Bell. He showed why he was a highly sought after recruit. It was easy to picture him becoming another spectacular running back at Wisconsin. South Jersey football had been good to the Wisconsin Badgers. Ron Dayne played his high school football at Overbrook in Pine Hill. Dayne won the 1999 Heisman Trophy and had a stellar NFL career for the New York Giants, Denver Broncos, and Houston Texans. The current Wisconsin running back, Corey Clement, was an All-American and expected to be an NFL draftee. Clement played his high school football for the Glassboro Bulldogs and set an opponent's single game rushing against Gloucester, carrying the ball for 479 yards against the Lions, at the time a New Jersey state high school rushing record in 2013. Bell scored on a 21-yard run with less than a minute left in the half. Salem headed to the locker room leading 28-22 at the half.

Oxley ran the second half kickoff to the Salem 33, and the Lions scored three plays later and regained the lead. Bell suffered leg cramps during the first series of Salem's offense. Without Bell in the backfield, the Lions defense stopped them on successive plays and forced them to punt. The Lions mounted a sustained drive and led 38-28 at the end of the third quarter. Bell returned to action in the fourth and scored after a long drive, cutting the Lions lead to 3. Oxley fumbled after a particularly hard hit from Bell on the Lions' next possession but Salem fumbled three plays later on a faulty snap from center. Oxley ran 37 yards before being driven out at the Salem 25. Miller connected with Mike King across the middle and the Lions escaped with a 46-42 victory. Bell had gained 301 yards on twenty-six carries. Oxley had gained 278 yards on thirty-one carries. Fans will be debating for years who was the better running back. The Lions were heading into their Thanksgiving showdown with Gloucester Catholic undefeated.

The Gloucester and Salem players shook hands at mid-field and the Lions headed for the end zone to listen to Coach Claiborn:

"Great effort by a great group of kids. I'm really proud of you guys. I don't think there were three opponents all year who weren't bigger or more talented than us. You guys have scratched and clawed your way to an 8-0 record. There is not a team anywhere I'd rather be standing in front of.

"I want to single somebody out at this point. I've seen players in the past who didn't have half of John Oxley's talent become completely intoxicated because they were getting attention from college football programs, Oxley's received letters from just about every major program in the country. Know how many he's opened so far? None. They're all sitting in bags in my office.

"I say that because it proves a point: you guys have, to a man, kept your complete focus on the task at hand. Nobody's gotten inflated. You came out every single day at practice and got right to work. You've kept out of trouble both in school and in the city. You've done every single thing anyone could ask you to do. We've got one more game to go. We'll be the underdog, but we've been the underdog four or five times already this season, including tonight. It shows that people underestimate our heart.

"We're playing Gloucester Catholic on Thanksgiving like we have for the past seventy-five years or so. Let me give you good advice about how to handle the buildup to this game. Do not get into any fights or arguments with anyone before or after the game. If you happen to run into any kids from their school in Wawa or Dunkin' Donuts, be quiet and respectful. We are doers. Leave the talking for the talkers. Don't bite the bait. There's certain people who'd love to see a Gloucester High kid overreact. Stay off of social media. I cannot emphasize that enough. Stay away from social media this week. We will let our actions do the talking on Thanksgiving. Let's walk together just a little further."

The Lions players were jubilant. They had answered the bell after every round so far. The biggest battle lay ahead. Gloucester Catholic was the number one-ranked team in South Jersey. Gloucester High was ranked number eight, their highest ranking in twenty years. Both schools had long, glorious histories on the gridiron. Both were well-coached. Both schools had a rabid fan base. Neither could imagine losing on Thanksgiving.

Gloucester Catholic's identity was equal parts Catholic spirituality and athletic dominance. It is a challenge for a Catholic school to remain open, let alone thrive, in the twenty-first century. The high schools throughout the greater

Philadelphia area struggled to maintain enrollment in the face of escalating tuition costs. The high schools were no longer viewed by diocesan bureaucrats as missions that deserved financial subsidies because they were cultivating the next generation of Catholics. Schools were forced to run as independent businesses that were responsible for paying their bills, fixing their aging buildings, and recruiting enough students to balance the accounting ledgers at the end of each year. Any school that couldn't operate as a financially feasible entity was summarily closed. Gloucester Catholic competed for students with two Catholic high schools that were situated in comfortable middle-class suburbs—Camden Catholic in Cherry Hill, and Paul IV in Haddon Township. Gloucester Catholic had made a wise decision in the 1980s to brand their school around their athletic teams, as Notre Dame University had done so successfully for decades. Gloucester Catholic had maintained healthy enrollment numbers by recruiting football players and baseball players and by appealing to kids who wanted the excitement of cheering for and sitting in class with promising (and potentially future professional) athletes.

The Rams had the best scholastic baseball program in the state and had a number of former players on major league rosters such as Bob Sebra, Zach Braddock, and Greg Burke. Their girls basketball program was the most storied girls high school athletic program in New Jersey, having won ten state championships. Even their ice hockey program was super successful and counted NHL superstar Johnny Gaudreau as an alum. Any season their football team wasn't undefeated was viewed as a disappointment. Their team drew loud, raucous crowds of devoted alumni and students each and every week. It wasn't unusual for a national caliber college football coach to speak at the Rams end-of-the-year sports banquet in late spring. A few college coaches had even solicited the opportunity to speak at the Rams banquet, hoping to make a favorable impression on their younger football players. The Rams were a football juggernaut. This season was expected to a potential letdown because the program had suffered major losses to graduation last year, sending graduates to Michigan, Temple, North Carolina, New Hampshire, and Mount Union. But here they were, as usual, at the top off the heap.

Gloucester City had many families whose allegiances were divided between the two schools. Most kids in Gloucester attended Gloucester High, but a sizable number had attended Gloucester Catholic through the years, often scattered from generation to generation; so the alumni were often friends with graduates of the other school. They fished together. They coached their children in youth sports together. They attended church together. They were invited to each other's celebrations and Baptisms and weddings.

But the week before Thanksgiving, nearly all of them realigned with graduates of the high school from which they graduated. Certain restaurants became the staging ground for Rams alumni. Other restaurants and bars catered to the Gloucester High crowd. Houses proudly displayed blue and gold Gloucester Lions flags or maroon and gold Gloucester Catholic Rams flags. A careless remark between cousins or even spouses could result in days of silence. Tempers flared. When there was still a Catholic grammar school in town, it wasn't unusual for ten-year-olds to be fist fighting on the way home from school. The newspapers referred to the rivalry as "The Holy War." The Wednesday night before the Thanksgiving game rivaled only New Year's Eve and St. Paddy's Night for the volume of drinking and partying that went on at the many bars and taverns in the city. Extra police were put on duty. The Thanksgiving game kicked off at 10:30 Thanksgiving morning and it was not uncommon for fans from either school to stagger up to the stadium gate directly from the previous night's revelry. Purse-lipped wives scanned the crowd looking for husbands who never came home from "meeting friends for a couple of drinks" the night before.

Because the game was played on Thursday, the Lions watched films of the Salem game on Saturday and practiced on Sunday for the first time that season. The Board of Education had granted permission for the team to practice as long as all scheduled Sunday church services were completed. Consequently, practice began at 2:00. The players didn't wear pads. The coaches demonstrated the defensive adjustments that the Lions planned to attempt to counteract the powerful Gloucester Catholic offense. Jeff Jackson was back at full strength. Gloucester Catholic played their home games on Saturdays at Gloucester High's football field, so nearly every Lions player had seen the Rams play in person this season. After the light practice, the team went into the classroom to watch films of Gloucester Catholic. The coaches presented an overview of strategies to stop the Rams. Their tone was respectful but optimistic. The film session lasted until 4:30.

Oxley had promised himself that he would minimize contact with Devan until after the Thanksgiving game. He rode home with Mike King and went into his house with every intention of spending the evening doing school work. He got a shower and wondered what to do for dinner because Joe's was closed on Sundays. At 5:30, his doorbell rang. It was Devan.

"Hey, Devan," Oxley greeted her as he opened the door.

"I really have to talk with you, Oxley. It's important."

"I can't do anything much, Dev. It's a big week coming up."

"That's why I'm here. We have to talk."

Oxley led her into the living room and sat at the very end of his sofa. Devan sat down and Oxley slid over another inch or two.

"If you slide down any more, Oxley, you'll be sitting on the arm of the sofa. I'm not going to bite you. Promise."

"Things do get carried away sometimes, Dev."

"Never when you're sober, Oxley. Sorry to break that news to you."

"Ayyyeee."

"Let's not fight. We're allies. I need to explain something to you. Please don't interrupt me."

"Right now, Devan? Do you know what this week is?"

"Oxley, there hasn't been a good time to tell you. I'm placing myself in great jeopardy telling you now."

"But…"

"Shhhh. This is more important than your football game. I know how you became this big football star, Oxley. I know McGrogan."

Oxley paled. He took a few deep breaths and struggled to not interrupt her.

"He's a bad, bad man, Oxley. You struck a deal with the devil. You've told yourself all along probably that you'll just not sign the contract beyond the trial period, right? The only catch is that once the trial period expires, you've got terrible karma and even worse, McGrogan has no need for you anymore. Whoever's football ability you have will get it back, and you will become disposable. McGrogan couldn't care any less about you. You are a minor player in this scheme.

"McGrogan's working with the professional football player at the other end. It's part of what lured the football guy to make the deal in the first place. All he had to do was lay low for a hundred days, and he's better than ever. The guy at the other end gets his athleticism restored and you're stuck with his negativity. You're a magnet for all kinds of tragedy. Ever hear of bad luck? You're going to be able to write a book about it—if you live that long. You're going to go from being the most popular guy in Gloucester City to the least popular guy in Gloucester history. I don't know what will happen but I do know it will be relentlessly, scandalously negative. And your life is in serious jeopardy."

"What the frig should I do?"

"We've got to work out a plan. Forget the Gloucester Catholic game. You guys are going to get your asses kicked. McGrogan timed that contract to end right at kickoff on Thanksgiving. I say this with all due respect, Oxley, but you are going to be good for absolutely nothing. You're going to be stuck with your old ability, or should I say, your old lack of ability."

"Should I sign the contract? I don't see how I have anything to lose."

"Only your soul. Don't count on being a college football star. It's a zero sum game. McGrogan lies and leads you on until he finally doesn't because you are no longer of any use to him. That day is fast approaching. The football player gets back his football and athletic skills. You'll be restored to the John Oxley who was walking home from rehearsing with Barb. Sign the contract and you might become a minor operative like me, used to help set up the next sucker that McGrogan needs for his next dirty deed. Or you might just meet some tragic end if he doesn't have any use for a brainy seventeen-year-old sax player."

"What's your story?"

"All you need to know about my story is that I am very sorry that I betrayed you a couple of times when I first got here. I hope I've made amends in the meantime. I'm a dead girl walking, but I realized that life isn't worth living without free will. I took back my free will and it will likely cost me my life. That's the choice you'll be stuck with, too."

"What do we do?"

"There's nothing you can do. Go to school. Go to practice. I have to figure out a plan. He's a demon. As long as he's around and operating, we are in grave danger. Let's meet Tuesday at six at Joe's."

Oxley asked Mike King to drop him off at Joe's on Tuesday after practice. Oxley walked in and saw Devan sitting in a booth checking her cell phone.

"Is this seat taken?" Oxley asked.

"I've lost my sense of humor," Devan said.

"Have you figured out what we can do?"

"It's a longshot, but yeah, I have a plan."

Just then, the door swung open and McGrogan walked to the booth where Devan and Oxley sat.

"Well, well, well, together under one roof—the former wallflower from Asheville and the saxophone wizard with the sluggish libido. Fast friends, I gather. Mind if I sit down?"

Oxley and Devan remained silent.

"I don't hear any of that '60s one-hit-wonder music, Oxley. Was this a business meeting I walked in on? You guys thinking about opening your own pizza steak place on the other side of Gloucester? Devan, I was hoping to have a word with the big running back. Your job is pretty much finished, right? Why don't you take a ride to the Jersey shore or somewhere? I'm thinking you'll be transferring out of state somewhere by the end of the week. Why don't you go see if you can win one last stuffed bear from one of those Wildwood boardwalk barkers?"

"It's November. The boardwalk's deserted."

"Even the slalom ride on Morey's Pier?"

"I'm leaving. Be careful, Oxley."

"How noble of you to care for young John like that. But Oxley's a big guy. We need to have a man-to-man talk, me and John."

Devan walked out without looking back.

"Let's get down to the real nitty gritty, junior. You've had a pretty nice run. On Labor Day, you were some geeky band guy who tenaciously stuck with football despite a singular lack of talent. By Thanksgiving, I've managed to transform you to the finest high school running back in New Jersey. But the roller coaster ride comes to an end on Thursday morning, right about kickoff time. At that time, you reclaim your paltry athletic skills, make a complete ass of yourself in front of the entire city, get demolished by Gloucester Catholic, scare away every single college coach from sea to shining sea, lose the girl—oh, excuse me, you and your sluggish libido have already managed to do that—and be persona non grata in Gloucester City like no one since the herpes outbreak of 1989. Or you can sign the contract, be the all-time football hero for the Gloucester Lions, take a few penthouse suite-level recruiting visits to Alabama, Clemson, Ohio State, Michigan, and anywhere else you're interested, recreate the whole Oxley mania thing on a college campus somewhere, maybe play football on Sundays, maybe move back here and run for mayor, who knows? But you're at a crossroad, Oxley, and the right path seems pretty clear from where I'm sitting. What do you think?"

"I think you're full of it, McGrogan. What guarantee do I have that I'll maintain any of this athletic prowess after I sign?"

"Oxley, my son, you've enjoyed ninety-eight days of premium gasoline in a Cobra engine compared to your previous seventeen years riding a rusty tricycle uphill into gale force winds. You've no doubt by now noticed the difference. It feels vastly different inhabiting a body that can actually do something other than blow into a horn. I bet people have started losing at you differently, right? They no longer have pity in their eyes. They probably want to talk with you, hang out even, hoping that some of your mojo wears off on them. This is only the beginning. These people are small town folks. Most of them haven't been any farther than Philadelphia. Imagine after you perform similar feats of brilliance at the Rose Bowl, the Cotton Bowl, the Orange Bowl. Even if you didn't ever play pro football, companies will hire you just to golf with the senior partners. Your life transforms from a bed of weeds to a bed of roses. Easy Street—ever hear of it?"

"What guarantee do I have?"

"No guarantee, numbnuts. Nobody on this whole planet gets a guarantee that they'll wake up tomorrow. It's a roll of the dice for a very big payoff. Life transforming, if I may say so myself."

"I thought the football guy was finished serving his suspension, that you'd be transferring his ability back."

"There'll probably be another guy looking for me tomorrow, junior. Domestic violence. Cocaine busts. Deflating footballs. I'm the top Karma Cleaner in this hemisphere. Like my business card reads, 'Quick. Quiet. Confidential.'"

Oxley was perplexed.

"When do I have to give you my answer?"

"I've heard through the grapevine that your favorite restaurant here is open for breakfast Thanksgiving morning. A chance for the drunks to get some waffles before cheering on the Blue and Gold. How about I give you the contract to peruse for a couple of days, you sign it, and Dame Devan drops it off to me right at this very booth, say, nine o'clock Thanksgiving morning. Tell her to look for the guy with the Crimson Tide hoodie."

The day before Thanksgiving is a dead zone for education pretty much anywhere in the country. At the high school at 1300 Market Street in Gloucester City, New Jersey, spirits were so high about the Thanksgiving football game that teaching was impossible. The hallways had been decorated by the Pep Club with hand painted posters exhorting the Lions to victory. Every player had a poster of a Lions football helmet painted with his name on it hanging on the wall outside his homeroom. Teachers offered players their encouragement. There was very little doubt among the students and the adults in the building that the Lions would emerge victorious the following morning.

Objective observers, such as sportswriters, saw things a little differently. Want Ad Wally, a pseudonym for *Courier-Post* sports writer Walt Mason, offered his prognostications all season on the South Jersey football games each week. He was remarkably accurate and correctly predicted about eighty percent of the outcomes each week. Want Ad Wally's predictions ran in the want ad section of the paper. He selected the Lions versus Rams Thanksgiving contest as the "Game of the

Week" and offered these insights in the Wednesday edition of the newspaper:

> *"The Lions have been South Jersey's Cinderella team this season. Expectations have risen every week as the Blue and Gold defeated one opponent after another, led by the area's premier running back, John Oxley. The perennial power Gloucester Catholic Rams have also exceeded predictions, running the table once again despite suffering heavy losses to graduation. Willie says the Lions' roller coaster ride finally comes to an end on Turkey Day.*
> *Final score Rams 35- Lions 21."*

The Lions practiced for the final time of the season after school ended. No one wore pads. It was a Gloucester High tradition for the players to wear their Gloucester midget league jerseys over a t-shirt to the final practice. They ran through their plays and were reminded again about the Rams offensive and defensive tendencies. The practice was enthusiastic and efficient. It ended the way the final practice ended each season in Gloucester—with the underclassmen carrying the seniors off the practice field for the final time on their shoulders. The mood was lighthearted and buoyant. The players gathered around the coaches in the center of the locker room.

Coach Claiborn said:

"All right, guys. We're at the castle gate. It took a lot of blood, sweat, and tears to get here. Let's go over what we have to do to finish the job tomorrow. First, no stupid penalties.

We've played penalty-free football all season. That's a big reason we've been so successful. We don't beat ourselves. The penalties that are most self-destructive are unsportsmanlike conduct and unnecessary roughness. Those penalties don't show toughness; they show a lack of discipline. If you are focused on winning, be aggressive and disciplined, and I want to emphasize the disciplined part. It comes from within. Stop when the whistle blows. Get focused on our next play. People might try to encourage you to be extra aggressive tomorrow but none of those people are playing the game. Be smart. Stay focused. Stay disciplined.

"Get some rest tonight. Turn off your minds, and get good sleep. Eat a smart breakfast. We're not used to playing in the morning, so make sure you have something to eat. Food is fuel. Smart, focused, disciplined.

"Tomorrow you'll take our field for the final time with your brothers who have fought side by side with you all season. Feel that connection out there tomorrow. We know what we have to do to win. We are a better football team. Let the papers, the sportswriters, all the know-it-alls pick the Rams. It's going to make it that much sweeter tomorrow after we beat them. We've had to claw and fight and scrap all year. We know what we have to do tomorrow.

"To the seniors, thanks for all you've given to Gloucester football. Nobody appreciates what you've done more than me. You are warriors. Lead the charge tomorrow. Underclassmen, let's send these guys out the way they deserve to go out—as champions.

"Finally—and there is no good time to announce this so I will tell you guys first—this is going to be my final game, too. I've never enjoyed a season as much as I've enjoyed this one. Let's keep that just with us until after the game tomorrow. Believe me, I've never wanted to win a game in my life, as a player or coach, as much as I want to win tomorrow. Bring in your hands."

The kids cried. The assistant coaches cried. Coach Claiborn remained steady and continued:

"Take a look at this town on your way home tonight and on your way to the stadium tomorrow. Think about what we stand for, what this school stands for, what this town stands for. It stands for not backing down. It stands for always showing up for the battle. It stands for refusing to be intimidated by any other man. We're going to carry this city in our hearts onto that field tomorrow. And I'll tell you right now, Gloucester Catholic doesn't stand a chance."

Oxley rode home in silence with Mike King. He texted Devan as soon as he was in his house.

"Wish I could spend the night focusing on the game tomorrow but I guess I can't. Can you pick me up?"

"I figured you'd want to meet for dinner so I came right to Joe's. Can you walk around? And can you bring that contract that McGrogan gave you?"

"On my way. I'll be right there. A lot went on at football."

Oxley walked into the pizzeria and glanced at the booth where he usually at with Devan. She wasn't there. He texted her:

"Didn't you say to meet at Joe's? I don't see you." Before he could send the message he looked up and saw Devan standing at the pizza counter in the back talking to Nick. When Devan heard his footsteps approaching, she spun around.

"Hey Oxley."

"Oxley-boyyyyyy."

"Hey Nick. Hey Devan."

"Let's go sit in the booth."

"Why were you back at the pizza counter?"

"Personal business."

"With Nick?"

"I said 'personal' business, as in *my* business, not yours. How was practice?"

"Spirited. Sad."

"Sad? How can football practice be sad?"

"Well, I can tell you because you're the only person in Gloucester that won't give a shit. Coach Claiborn is retiring from coaching after tomorrow's game."

"All things must pass. Let's get down to non-football related items. What are you going to do about signing or not signing the contract?"

"What are my options, in your opinion? Turns out you know McGrogan a lot better than I do."

"Your options are all bad. Don't sign the contract and you'll lose your amped-up athletic skills as soon as the game begins. Whatever adjustments he made to you will expire one hundred days to the minute from the time he set them. And that's just the beginning of your troubles. Your life will be in jeopardy, and my life will be in jeopardy. He won't run the risk of you being around to tell anyone what actually happened a hundred days ago. You're as disposable as a toothbrush, Oxley. He's not the sentimental type."

"What's he gonna do, shoot me after the game?"

"He's not bound by the laws of physics. I thought you were smart."

"Shit."

"Yeah, 'shit.'"

"So if you don't sign it, you're as vulnerable as I am now that he knows I've betrayed him."

"If I do sign it?"

"You have your big, bad football game and then you become a minor functionary like I am. You'll be used as bait in bigger, better schemes. You might be in high school the next ten years. Imagine that. You'll be told who to flirt with, who to hang out with, and so on. It's like that movie *Groundhog Day*, except it isn't funny. He will promise you whatever he thinks it will take to get you to sign. Then there will be endless diversions and excuses. Best-case scenario is that you get to continue the football thing at the college level but you have no free will from the moment you sign that contract. You're dancing to his tune until he doesn't need you any longer."

"I ain't signing it. I can't believe what a mess I'm in."

"You were gullible and have an ego just like everyone else."

Oxley pulled the contract out of his pocket and tore it to pieces.

"Here."

"I've got something cooking. He's always underestimated me. I'm going down swinging. You go about your night as if none of this happened. It's been good knowing you. Hope you beat the Rams or whoever tomorrow."

"The Rams. Will I ever see you again?"

"Highly doubtful. And please don't have a breakdown over me like you did Barb. Some guys love them and leave them. You're the only guy in the world who leaves them, then loves them. If you survive this mess, get some therapy."

Oxley sighed and extended his hand.

"Thanks, Devan. For everything."

"Go practice your saxophone, dude."

Thanksgiving morning, Devan went to Joe's shortly before 9:00 and waited for McGrogan. The Pizzeria was already boisterous. It had been too many years since the Lions had a chance to compete with Gloucester Catholic and the Lions diehards who frequented Joe's were buoyant. They sat, as they always did, Pop Sullivan, Ott Romeo, Nick Brown, and Bob Cooney in booths, and Bud Lindsay and the Yula brothers sitting in the seats that lined the counter. Devan nodded to them on the way in and sat alone in a booth at the end until McGrogan strolled in at exactly 9:00. He wore a grey Alabama Crimson Tide hoodie with a giant red elephant on the chest. He had his well-worn "Karma's a Bitch" cap on his head and an ear-to-ear grin. He sat across from Devan and said, "Break it to me gently, sweetheart. What's Little Lord Oxley's decision?"

Devan uncapped her hand and the shreds of the torn-up contract poured onto the table in front of McGrogan.

"You're both goners," was all he said to her as he grabbed the bits of paper in one quick motion and spun to address the Gloucester guys.

"Any betting men among you? I'll give you Gloucester and ten. No, make it fourteen. The Rams might win by forty. This one's gonna be over by halftime, mark my word. How about a few wagers to spice things up a bit?"

Devan left quickly and by the time she pulled her car around the corner at 9:05, Nick was drawing the blinds to close the place for the day. Thanksgiving is not a big day for pizza, even in Gloucester. Game time was 10:30.

Coach Claiborn and his assistants were in the coaches' room by 7:00. A few players were waiting outside the locker room when the coaches arrived. Players were required to arrive by 8:45 to dress. If a player needed to be taped or to see the trainer, they must arrive by 8:15. Players had individual superstitions about wearing certain socks, t-shirts, the order in which they put on their equipment, and how they taped their spikes. Metallica blared through the locker room speakers until 8:55, when the quarterbacks, receivers, and linemen had breakout meetings with their respective assistant coaches. At 9:05, the entire team gathered to hear the defensive coordinator review the day's game plan. Coach Claiborn then reviewed the offensive game plan. Each game of the season, Coach Claiborn outlined five or six goals that must be accomplished if the Lions were to be successful that day. Specialists went outside to begin warming up at 9:25—the punters, long snappers, place kickers, quarterbacks, and receivers. Coach Claiborn went out to the field with them and the assistant coaches remained in the locker room with the rest of the Lions team. At 9:55, the remainder of the team came out to the field to stretch. The assistant coaches worked with their charges until 10:10. At that time, the Lions reentered the locker room. They had five minutes to get a drink and to use the lav. At 10:15, Coach Claiborn gave one final motivational talk, and at 10:25, he led the captains out to the field for the coin toss.

The Rams won the toss and elected to kick off. They squibbed the kick and a Gloucester lineman fell on the ball at the Lions 37-yard line. Guessing that the Rams defense would try to make a statement on the opening play by stuffing Oxley, the Lions faked a handoff to him and threw to their sophomore wide receiver Don Demeter streaking down the right sideline. The call was astute. The Rams blitzed on first down to stop Oxley, and the pass was completed to a wide open Demeter for a 63-yard touchdown strike. Lions fans were delirious. The stadium quaked with excitement and the Lions mobbed Demeter in the end zone. The cheering from the Lions stands was deafening. People were still filing into the stadium and had to ask what had just happened. What had they missed? Even the guys from Joe's were late getting to the field.

When people told them what happened, Nick said, "No shit!"

It was a great moment to be wearing blue and gold. But in that minute of excitement, and with their eyes focused on Demeter in the end zone, watching him walk with his teammates back to the Lions sideline, hardly anyone had noticed the writhing figure of John Oxley lying at the 30-yard line. The stadium hushed, the Rams fans out of respect and the Lions out of worry. The Lions team doctor, Dr. Carl Viscenzo, sprinted out onto the field. He was accompanied by the Lions trainer, two Rowan University sports medicine interns, and the Lions coaches. As the crowd grew quiet, they say that even fans at the far end of the stadium near the basketball pavilion could hear Oxley scream out in pain. He was gasping when Dr. Viscenzo arrived.

"My leg. My knee. I felt a pop in my knee but that's not what's killing me. I think my leg's broken."

Dr. Viscenzo examined Oxley's leg and his single, worried glance back at Coach Claiborn confirmed everyone's worst fear. Oxley's tibia was broken in two spots. Further examination at the Cooper Hospital would reveal that he had suffered a torn ACL and a torn MCL. There is an ambulance on duty at every Gloucester football game, and the Lions trainer waved the EMTs onto the field. The stadium remained eerily quiet. Oxley's leg was immobilized and his teammates gathered at a respectful distance. Oxley was crying. As the EMTs strapped Oxley to a stretcher, his teammates touched his head or the rail of the stretcher.

"We got this, buddy."

"Hang in there, Oxley."

Mike King approached him as the men collapsed the wheels to lift him into the back of the ambulance.

"We're gonna bring you the game ball after we win this thing, kid."

The ambulance pulled gingerly past the crowd that had gathered at the gate, drove slowly over the speed bumps in the Gloucester High parking lot, and then sped down Route 130 to Cooper Hospital in neighboring Camden. Back inside the stadium, the teams and fans reoriented themselves to the football contest. Extra points often seem anticlimactic, yet this one felt surreal. The Lions placekicker, Chris Foster, was called on for the first time this season to do something besides launch booming kickoffs. Foster split the uprights, and the Lions led 7-0. The remainder of the first quarter was played between the 30-yard lines. Neither team could mount any kind of sustained drive, and the quarter ended with the Lions clinging to their 7-0 lead.

Gloucester Catholic showed their mettle in the second quarter. They ran back a punt to the Lions 29-yard line and scored five plays later. Their offensive line dominated the line of scrimmage. A Gloucester drive petered out after picking up one first down, and the Rams scored another touchdown right before halftime. The score at the half was Gloucester Catholic 14-Gloucester 7.

The Lions tried an onside kick to begin the second half and caught the Rams napping. The Lions needed a defensive holding call against the Rams to keep this drive alive and punched one in on fourth and goal from the 1. Foster's extra point knotted the score at 14. The crowd roared with every play. The tie was short-lived as the Rams struck back, methodically chewing up yardage on a series of runs and short passes, scoring on a quick hit over the middle with a minute left in the third quarter. The Rams gambled on going for two on the extra point but were stopped when their running back lost his footing and slipped before the play had a chance to develop. The score stood at 20-14 in favor of the Rams. The third quarter drew to a close with the Lions facing a third and 5 from their own 32-yard line.

The crowd was completely riveted on every play. A roar went up as the two teams took the field to begin the fourth quarter. There were still twelve minutes remaining in the game, but a feeling prevailed among Lions fans that it was critical that they score. Their defense did not appear capable of stopping the Rams offense. On the third and 5, the Lions handed the ball to their halfback who faked a run and then stepped back to attempt a pass. He found Mike King all alone 20 yards over the middle, and the big tight end carried the ball to the Rams 20 before he was brought down. It took the Lions six plays but they struck pay-dirt when Mergens carried the ball over from the 3. Foster's third extra point staked the Lions to a 21-20 lead with just over nine minutes to play.

The Lions kicked deep and the Rams returned the ball to the 30. Gloucester Catholic had relied on their running game to this point and startled the Lions defense by picking up first downs on consecutive pass completions. The Rams were in Lions territory with eight minutes to go. A succession of runs over right tackle brought the ball to the Lions 15. The Rams picked up a first down on three more running plays. They had the ball first and goal from the Gloucester 4-yard line. It took two tries but the Rams found the end zone. They gambled again on a two-point conversion but again they were unsuccessful. The Rams led 27-21.

The time on the clock read 4:59. The crowd remained raucous as the Rams prepared to kick off. The kickoff was covered perfectly by the Rams, and the Lions were pinned deep in their own territory with the clock ticking. The Lions ran for a first down and passed for another. Mergens got around the end for a 12-yard gain but fumbled at the end of the play. After a lengthy debate, it was ruled that he fumbled on contact with the ground and the Lions had a first and 10 at midfield. Just over two minutes remained.

The crowd was deafening and the Lions struggled to hear their signals. They attempted a pass on first down that was nearly intercepted. A second down run gained 3 and the Lions were facing third and long. A misdirection play picked up the first down but the Blue and Gold were 40 yards from the end zone with just two minutes remaining.

Everyone in the large crowd stood and screamed for their boys. The snack stands hastily closed so the workers could see the final minutes. The Lions ran the ball twice for no gain. They faced another third and long. The Rams defense appeared energized even after forty grueling minutes. The Lions quarterback Denny Miller faked a handoff to Mergens and stepped back to pass. He found his receivers covered and sensed the Rams linemen closing in on him. He ran out of the pocket to escape the pass rush and found an opening down the sidelines, scampering for 15 yards until he was driven out of bounds at the 25. The play stopped the clock with forty-seven seconds left in the football game. Gloucester had two time outs remaining. The Lions passed on first down but only picked up 6 on the play. They quickly called time out. The ball was on the Rams 19 with thirty-nine ticks of the clock remaining.

Most of the crowd had forgotten that it was Thanksgiving and were screaming with primal urgency, exhorting their kids to prevail. Everyone lived in the moment, completely focused on the playing field. Denny Miller handed the ball to Mergens, who pitched it right back to him and Miller hit sophomore wide receiver Shane Smith up the sideline. Smith juked one defender but was driven out of bounds at the 7, stopping the clock with twenty-nine seconds remaining. On first down, the Lions ran a counter for a gain of 1 yard. The Lions ran another play immediately and gained 4 yards as Mergens bulled his way to the 2. The Lions called their final time out. There were eight seconds remaining in the game.

Fans screamed and prayed and yelled encouragement to their teams. Eight seconds was all that stood between agony for one squad and ecstasy for the other. The timeout ended and the refs signaled for play to resume. The clock would start on the snap. Miller approached the line of scrimmage and began the signals. The hopes of thousands rested on a play between twenty-two teenage boys. Miller faked a handoff to Mergens, pivoted, and passed to Eric McDonough, who was running a fade route to the far right corner of the end zone. The pass somehow eluded the arms of a couple of Ram defenders and McDonough grabbed it spinning and soaring above his head. He landed with both feet in the corner of the end zone and looked up to the heavens.

The Lions had won the biggest victory in Gloucester High history. McDonough was mobbed by his teammates on the field, then by the remainder of his team and his coaches, then by an army of Gloucester fans who stampeded the field from the stands. They hoisted Eric onto their shoulders and carried him back to the sidelines. The refs had run for the safety of the locker room. The traditional postgame handshake was impossible because of the pandemonium on the field. The Rams coach graciously found Coach Claiborn and offered his congratulations. The Lions had finished the season undefeated. Veteran sportswriter Phil Rocabaldo of the *Philadelphia Inquirer* called the game "the most exciting high school athletic contest I've covered in my forty years as a reporter. An absolute epic that will be replayed, debated and celebrated for as long as these two great schools are standing."

Lions fans were patiently asked to leave the playing field by the host of police officers who had volunteered to provide security that day. Finally, the Gloucester football team was alone together in the end zone. Mr. Powell led the singing of "That Ol' Gloucester Spirit." None of the coaches could talk without getting immediately choked up. Pandemonium still reigned everywhere else in the city but life became very still for the kids kneeling on one knee in their end zone. Coach Claiborn cut his speech to a single sentence:

"We did it."

Then he was mobbed and carried off the field on his players' shoulders. They carried him to the front of the locker room and went inside to celebrate among themselves while he spoke with reporters.

"Dreams don't always come true," he told them. "That's a lesson life teaches us over and over. The bigger the dream, the less likely you'll realize it. This was a big dream. In competitive sports, a hundred coaches begin the season with the same dream and only one gets to see it realized. From the very first practice, these kids were concerned with only one goal—winning. They didn't care who got the credit, who was in the newspaper, who was mentioned on social media; if we won, that was enough. Period. Their only concern after one win was what we had to do to earn another. They did not allow themselves to become distracted by things they couldn't control and kept their focus completely on things that could be controlled—their effort, the strategies we came up with each week, eating right, staying hydrated, getting plenty of rest—all the little things that get you the big things. I'm proud as can be that I can walk into the same locker room with so many humble kids. The words 'humble' and 'champion' haven't been used together much lately, but these kids are the epitome of both."

The locker room was a swirling circus. Kids lingered, not wanting to disconnect from the bond that had brought them so close. Finally, after their parents' texts become increasingly impatient, players started to leave, hugging each other one final time before joining their families for Thanksgiving dinners. The coaches said goodbye to each other and planned to meet the next day to review the film. The game would be on Hudl by this evening. Coach Claiborn drove to the hospital with the game ball before heading home. Cooper Hospital was only a ten-minute drive from Gloucester. He received a pass from the security guard and headed to Room 409. He spotted Oxley laying with his leg immobilized before he entered the room.

"Nice digs, dude."

"Hey, Coach. Congratulations!"

"I guess you heard, huh?"

"People were texting me every thirty seconds. It was worse than the busted leg! I was in agony waiting to see if we won."

"How bad's the leg?"

"Broken tibia. Torn ACL and MCL. Badly bruised fibula. Going to be laid up for a while. I'm happy we won."

"Wasn't easy without you, buddy."

"It's weird, but I'm glad it turned out the way it did. I'm glad you won without me."

"You're the craziest guy I ever coached, Johnny."

"It makes me feel good that you guys did it without me. We were never a one-man team."

"No, we weren't. You were smart enough to realize that. What am I going to tell all the colleges that call?"

"Ask them if they have any scholarships for a saxophone guy in their marching band."

"Some of the football guys might be willing to wait the year and redshirt you."

"No thanks. My football career is over. In some ways I'm relieved. I loved playing for Gloucester, but you know I was on the fence about playing in the future."

"Like I said, you're the craziest guy I ever coached. Here's the game ball, buddy. Everybody signed it. You brought a lot of magic to the program this year."

"We're going out together, Coach. Did you tell the reporters yet?"

"No, I don't want to sidetrack the story about the game. I'll tell everybody in a few days."

Oxley extended his hand.

"Thanks for everything, Coach. I'm grateful for so much these past four years. Just as grateful for the first three years as this one. I'm a way better person for it."

"And I'm a better man, too, buddy, for having had you around for four years. Everybody's going to come see you in a couple of days. Get some rest. Don't worry about the operation. These doctors can do it in their sleep they see so many of them."

They shook hands one more time and the coach went home to his family.

Oxley's mom brought him up Thanksgiving dinner, perfectly prepared turkey with all of the trimmings from Max's, a local restaurant. His mom spent two hours alternately crying because of the severity of his injuries and sharing his joy that that the Lions went undefeated. She kissed him goodbye and promised to be back at 8 the next morning. Oxley dozed off watching music videos on his phone. Around 8:00, someone poked him in the ribs. He glanced up and saw Barb.

"Hey, jerko," she said.

"Hey, Barb. Whew! What a day!"

"I cried like a baby when you got hurt. A bunch of people were crying."

"I feel better just seeing you. Guess I should have broken my leg sooner."

Barb was wearing a Mission of Burma t-shirt, yoga pants, and pink Ugg Bailey Button Bling boots. She wore a zip up Thrasher hoodie over the t-shirt.

"Wouldn't be much of a friend if I didn't visit you. I heard you're seriously hurt. Do you need an operation?"

"In the morning."

"Darn, dude. I told you football's too crazy."

"I remember you saying that."

"What else do you remember?"

"I remember how much I looked forward to seeing you every day. I remember how much we have in common. How beautiful I think you are. How much of a void I felt once we disconnected."

"I miss you, Oxley."

"I miss you. More than I ever realized I could miss anyone."

"Jeez. I'm sorry I acted stupid. I felt threatened by Devan."

"I've learned a lot."

"Really? Tell me something you've learned." She ran her fingernails up and down his arm.

"That I love you."

She began to cry, unlatched the side of the safeguard, and slid into the bed beside him.

"I love you, Oxley. I've been holding my breath for weeks now trying to figure out a way to crawl back to you without completely losing face with everyone."

"I thought we weren't ever going to worry about what other people thought."

"In that case, you're stuck with me."

McGrogan was never seen in Gloucester again, and Oxley never once heard from him. The town celebrated the Thanksgiving victory until almost Christmas, but McGrogan was nowhere to be found and never paid off the bets he made Thanksgiving morning at Joe's.

It was a particularly frigid February that winter and the thin swath of Delaware River that stretched from Gloucester's riverfront to South Philadelphia froze over. Kids skated on the river for the first time in twenty years.

The river finally thawed at the end of March and men cleaning storm debris from the city marina found an Alabama Crimson Tide hoodie with a giant elephant on the chest floating in the river. After the National Championship football game in January, there were probably dozens of Crimson Tide hoodies tossed into rivers, dumpsters, and trash cans—except this one had a crumpled baseball cap inside the front pouch that read, "Karma's a Bitch."

51182338R00132

Made in the USA
Middletown, DE
08 November 2017